A Twist of Hate

T. E. LORENZO

5 PRINCE PUBLISHING

Copyright © 2023 by T. E. Lorenzo, A TWIST OF HATE

All rights reserved.

This is a fictional work. The names, characters, incidents, and locations are solely the concepts and products of the author's imagination, or are used to create a fictitious story and should not be construed as real. No part of this book may be reproduced in any form or by any electronic or mechanical means, including information storage and retrieval systems, without written permission from the author, except for the use of brief quotations in a book review.

Published by 5 PRINCE PUBLISHING & BOOKS, LLC

PO Box 865, Arvada, CO 80001

www.5PrinceBooks.com

ISBN digital: 978-1-63112-336-8

ISBN print: 978-1-63112-337-5

07032023

For Monita.
10 years strong and no slowing down.
I love you forever.

Acknowledgments

I owe a major thank you to the team at 5 Prince Publishing. Not only for seeing the potential in this story, but for helping make it everything it can be.

Thank you to Bernadette, my best friend in this wild industry, for taking a chance on a thriller writer trying to navigate the marathon of writing a romance. I am forever indebted to you for bringing this book to life.

A special thank you to Cate Byers, my editor on this book. You pushed me so far out of my comfort zone as a writer, I'm not sure I can find my way back. Not only did you help strengthen this story to become something readers will enjoy, you provided me with a crash course of new tools and considerations to add to my arsenal for future books. Still not sure I can handle all the dialogue tags. Ha!

I wrote this book in "secret" hoping to give it to my wife as a gift for our 10-year wedding anniversary. While not too many people knew about it, I need to thank everyone who helped keep this secret. It was no easy feat, but one that was totally worth it! Note to self: don't ever attempt to write a secret book again!

This was a fictionalized retelling of my wife and I's love story. Most of the events are true, even if placed somewhere else in the timeline of what really happened. That said, my last thank you is for my wife, Natasha. Thank you for going on that trip to Vegas. I can't imagine how things would have turned out if you hadn't.

A Twist of Hate

CHAPTER *One*

NATALIA STROLLED INTO THE OFFICE, bundled up thanks to the blustery, cold weather outside. She worked part time at Coors Field, home of the Colorado Rockies. They were all part time in the call center, one of the several cost-cutting strategies bestowed by ownership to prevent paying for health insurance for their employees.

But Natalia didn't care about any of that. She wasn't working to build a career in Major League Baseball. Rather, she had needed a job that provided flexibility to complete her thesis and last semester of earning her master's degree from the University of Colorado.

She had completed all the coursework back in December, followed by a month-long trip to visit family in Colombia—and to celebrate her graduation, of course.

Today was the final Friday of January, and she had started the search for her new job earlier in the week. She didn't go through the hell of earning her master's in structural engineering to sell baseball tickets over the phone for poverty wages.

The call center was fairly split between college students and retirees looking to pass the time—and get free tickets to eighty-one games of baseball each year. Natalia got along with just about everyone, developing friendships she liked to think would last a lifetime.

Even though it was Friday, it was Natalia's first day in the office that week, having taken the extra time off to apply for jobs and schedule interviews.

Job hunting should be classified as torture, she thought. *A whole week down the drain. For what? Five rejections, two non-responses, and one phone interview with a lousy firm.*

Natalia was ready for the next phase in life—a real career. She didn't hate working for the Rockies. They had provided her exactly what she needed for that final semester of college. But each passing day felt one step further from where she wanted to be. Angst clashed with her inner hunger for that coveted "grown up" job, and stepping into the call center each morning put an immediate damper on her mood.

She had made it this far, and could only hold on to her blind faith that it would all work out soon.

"Good morning, Denver," she said to the call center's most popular employee when she entered the break room to put her lunch box in the refrigerator.

"Morning, Natalia," he replied. Denver Wallace was one of the retirees, splitting two part-time jobs between the call center and as a suite attendant on game days, all in the name of adding to his Major League Baseball pension that had accrued over the past fifteen years. "Ready for another day in paradise?"

"You know it."

"How did the job hunt go?" he asked in a hushed tone, turning his attention to the coffee maker to brew a cup of hot chocolate.

Natalia had confided in Denver last week after he noticed her request for more time off shortly after returning from an extended vacation. It wasn't even much of a secret—Natalia had told her boss of her intentions to find new employment before the season started in April—but Denver understood plenty well how to play the corporate game and didn't want the wrong ears to catch wind of Natalia's plans.

"It was good," she lied. "Found lots of great companies. I think I sent out about fifteen applications. Probably a few more."

"I know you'll find the right one. You're a catch." He poured two cups of hot chocolate and handed one to Natalia.

"Thanks, Denver," she said, taking a sip and licking her lips with satisfaction. "We should probably head in before Lopez complains about us being late."

Denver rolled his eyes. "That guy."

Natalia left Denver in the breakroom, hot chocolate in hand and ready for the day. With everyone being part time, there was no saying who would work on a given day, especially in the off-season.

She strolled down a long hallway, passing by an open bullpen area where the season ticket team sat across from the enclosed elevator lobby.

"Good morning, Charles," she greeted one of the sales reps, continuing down the hall, smiling and nodding to the group ticketing department, their desks set up within two opposite alcoves in the hallway.

She reached the end of the hall where a long wall covered in stars celebrated all the employees of the month from the call center.

Not a wall my name will ever hang on. And that's fine.

Their office was tucked away, out of sight of anyone important. If the call center's doors had remained closed, people might just walk by and confuse it with a closet. It was an entry-level position meant to weed out the weak and provide a path for those —typically men—who were serious about a career in baseball.

Natalia stepped in, the usual morning silence filling the room. The call center had three long rows of desks, short dividers separating everyone's workspaces. A boxy TV was mounted high above the front row. The other two rows were walled off from the front with a ledge at chest level. They referred to their manager's office as the fishbowl, as it was on a slightly elevated platform at the rear of the room, a semicircle enclosed in glass.

Only seven of us working today. That should be enough for each of us to take four calls all day. I don't know why we're even open in January. At least it's free money, I suppose.

Her friend, Allyson, sat at the first desk next to the door, nose already buried in a book.

"Still reading that book?" Natalia asked, startling Allyson out of the fictional trance she had fallen into.

"Oh, hey Natalia! Yeah, I think I can finish before lunch—that's my goal."

"I'll leave you to it."

Seated in the row behind Allyson was Rick, his frosty white hair protruding over the top of the newspaper held wide in both hands. He flipped down the top half to reveal his blue eyes swimming behind a thick pair of glasses, fingerprints clouding every inch of the lenses.

"Natalia," Rick greeted. His voice always sounded like his tongue was picking something in the back of his mouth. "How's it going, kiddo?"

Rick and Denver were the best of friends, and she knew Denver had mentioned her job hunt to him.

"Hey, Rick," Natalia replied, taking her purse off her shoulder. "I'm glad to be back. How are you?"

"Oh, you know, another day in this paradise. I can't complain."

"It wouldn't be a paradise without you. How would we ever make it through the day without you making us laugh?"

Rick nodded to himself. "That is true."

He was a native New Yorker with no filter, and never shied away from heckling the customers who called in, treating everyone to multiple rounds of laughter each day.

Natalia continued along, the rest of the middle row empty for now.

"Hey, girl, hey!" said Melissa Wilson from the back row,

standing up with a wide smile to greet Natalia.

"Good morning!" Natalia said, shuffling toward her desk at the far end of the front row. Melissa loved to chat in the mornings, and today would be an extended session thanks to Natalia's vacation.

"How was all the time off?" Melissa asked.

Natalia turned on her computer and dropped her purse on her desk before walking around to stand in front of Melissa's post. "It was good. Productive."

"Oh?" Melissa asked, winking. She had also known what Natalia had been up to during her time away.

"Yes, girl. It went well."

"Good. You deserve it. I'll be praying for you." Melissa batted her eyelashes playfully.

"Thank you." Natalia offered a gentle smile to Melissa. "I need to finish getting set up for the day."

"Of course. We can totally catch up later."

Natalia returned to her desk and sorted her belongings. Her book was ready, phone and computer successfully logged into. Even the TV was still off—she hated when it blared first thing in the morning. All was primed for a perfect day.

Until Adrian walked in.

Oh great, Natalia thought. *Mr. Asshole himself decided to grace us with his presence today.* Almost *a perfect day.*

Natalia *hated* Adrian Gonzalez. Or was *despised* a better word? She couldn't recall someone treating her so disrespectfully, especially in an office environment.

For as much as they each got along with everyone else in the office, the two had never spoken a word to each other since Natalia started last summer. Six months without a word? They'd passed each other in the hall or break room plenty of times. Even ridden in the elevator together. But he never said a word to Natalia, never even smiled in her direction like a decent human might do.

Sure, Adrian had been working with the group ticketing

department when she had first started, so his time in the call center was limited. But he still wandered in daily to check in with Denver and Melissa, both of whom sat within ten feet of Natalia. He'd strike up conversations with everyone else during his visits, but acted like Natalia was invisible.

His time with the groups department meant he sat in the alcove directly outside the call center. Natalia passed by his desk at least a half dozen times every day. They'd usually make eye contact, and Adrian would promptly look back at his computer screen. Or, her favorite, he'd keep an intense gaze on his screen to avoid eye contact at all. It was these instances when she started wondering why Adrian went out of his way to act like she simply didn't exist.

And for someone who had been with the organization for four years, had worked in different departments, and was allegedly in the running for a team lead role in the call center, why would he not at least introduce himself to Natalia?

Natalia thought they might even form a bond, considering they were the only two Latinos in the office. It didn't mean they had to be friends, but it was enough to warrant a simple hello.

Adrian seemed to be liked by everyone, and the feeling reciprocated. Except for Natalia.

At first, she thought he was just shy and would take a couple of days to introduce himself. Then a few weeks passed, and she figured he was just laser-focused on his work—he was working with the group ticketing team at the time of her hiring. However, *months* passed and Adrian transferred back to the call center once the season ended, and he still never looked Natalia's way.

And so began the confusion which took little time evolving into a deep loathing.

Another day of being invisible to Mr. Asshole. If you danced on his desk, would he even look up?

It almost became a game they played—well, Natalia played—wondering when the magical day might come when Adrian would walk up and start a conversation. It *had* to happen at some point. You simply couldn't work with someone for an entire year and deny their existence right to their face. Adrian was at the water cooler at least six times a day, directly next to Natalia's desk. She had tried everything to see if he would make eye contact. Looking at the bulletin board behind him. Looking at the water cooler. Facing him directly. Even getting behind him in line for the water. Name it, and Natalia had tried it, to no avail.

She had even asked Melissa—who had been part of Adrian's starting class all those years ago—if she knew why he was treating her this way.

"It just takes him a while to open up to new people," Melissa had explained. She and Denver probably knew him best. Denver had given Natalia a similar response, coupled with, "You just have to start the conversation with Adrian. At least at first."

But Natalia couldn't allow herself to do that, not this late into the game. Part of her wanted to see if they could actually work an entire year together without speaking. Surely it had to be a record. Another part of her saw it as a challenge, trying to get him to speak to her. With the clock ticking down on her time working at the Rockies, she wondered if she could make him speak to her before her last day.

When that day came, would he say goodbye without having ever said hello? Would he confess to playing out some kind of experiment, which almost felt like what Natalia was doing at this point? Or would he just let her vanish out of his life, content with never speaking a single word to a fellow human being?

With college complete, Natalia considered figuring out Mr. Asshole the hardest task for the winter.

But they were in a game of chicken, apparently, and whoever spoke first lost. And Natalia was no loser.

You hate him because you can't figure him out. He's not mysterious. He's a riddle. Are there some riddles with no answer? This frustrated Natalia because she believed everything required a logical explanation. And this matter simply didn't have one.

She had been to plenty of different places where she might

spend a few hours near a person without speaking. But that never bothered her. She considered it rude, but didn't hold it against the offenders. But with Adrian, maybe it was the professional setting that set her up with different expectations. Not even she understood why she got so worked up about it.

None of that matters. He's an asshole. You're not. You have a good book to read. He has some strange Stephen King novel. Just go about your business today and let him live in his misery.

As if Adrian had been reading her thoughts, he strode away from his desk and rounded the corner behind Natalia, empty water bottle in hand, en route to the cooler. Natalia whipped open a crossword puzzle and leaned forward to scan the contents.

He continued straight ahead, tunnel vision on the water cooler. She knew she was in his line of vision, and casually glanced in his direction as one would naturally do.

Adrian bent forward, staring at his bottle like it might run away. His black hair was slicked to the side and his scent wafted into her nostrils. She hated the guy, sure, but could acknowledge he had won the battle against body odor.

Just look up, Mr. Asshole. Look at me, and I'll even smile at you.

She tried willing the words into his mind, as if that would make him suddenly realize she existed.

But he didn't. He returned to his desk without an acknowledgement.

Never fails, she thought. *Until next time, Mr. Asshole.*

CHAPTER *Two*

Natalia Ayala, Adrian thought. *Could there be a more unpleasant person in the world?*

When he walked into the office that morning, he had hoped for a stress-free day. And it would be, mostly. Rockies tickets weren't on sale yet. He never understood why they even bothered keeping the call center open from October through January—they literally had nothing to do.

Oh well, free money, I suppose. Gotta be able to buy my dollar menu dinners.

Adrian had worked in the Rockies call center for the past four years, all throughout college. The pay was atrocious. He had learned the meaning of living paycheck to paycheck. Almost all of his money went toward rent for the two-bedroom apartment he and his best friend lived in. After paying his share of the cable and utility bills, he'd be lucky to have an extra hundred dollars after each payday.

At least he had the free entertainment of Rockies games all summer long. Eighty-one events at his disposal. And whenever he invited a friend or relative to join him, they always bought him dinner as a thank you for the ticket.

Graduation loomed three months away, but Adrian had settled into a comfortable groove despite the measly pay.

"Morning, Denver," Adrian said, dropping his backpack on the floor under his desk. He was the furthest thing from a morning person and refused to say '*good* morning'. People never noticed he left off this one word, and that was fine in his book.

"Adrian," Denver said, peeling the foil lid off a container of yogurt. "How's it going?"

"Couldn't be better. I played in an online tournament last night—been trying to do that nightly, actually, to get some practice before Vegas. Ended up winning a hundred and fifty. I'll be putting that aside to take on the trip."

Despite an age difference of over forty years, they had become close friends. Denver had taken Adrian under his wing when he had first started in the call center. Denver knew *everyone* in the building and never shied away from offering advice to the several college-aged kids who came through the revolving door of the Colorado Rockies call center.

With Adrian, however, they connected on a more personal level. Their bond blossomed from a shared loved of baseball and poker, then flourished once they started spending time together outside of work. In time, they knew each other's families, and without saying it, Denver had always looked out for Adrian in both the professional and personal environments.

When Adrian had turned twenty-one a few weeks earlier, Denver offered to take him on a trip to Las Vegas in February. They were scheduled to fly out the afternoon following the big on-sale date, when tickets for all the Rockies games went on sale for the season ahead.

"One fifty?" Denver said. "Nice. What was the buy-in?"

"Three dollars. I can't exactly afford to risk much more than that."

A year prior, Adrian had watched the World Series of Poker for the first time, and witnessed with awe as twenty-one-year-old Joe Cada overcame a field of over six thousand players to win eight million dollars in prize money. Having long thought of the game as gambling, he quickly understood the intense level of skill and patience required to succeed in poker.

On his actual birthday, Adrian had no interest in going out to bars to have his first legal drink. He went to the casinos in Black Hawk instead, spending the day learning how to play live poker, blackjack, roulette, and craps, games that would become some of his favorite hobbies.

"As of last night," Denver said. "Everything is officially booked for the trip. Hotel and flights. Were you able to find a schedule of poker tournaments?"

"Yes. There are so many, but I narrowed it down to a few we can check out."

"Good. I want to play in one every day if we can. If not, lots of blackjack."

"Consider it done." Adrian slapped the top of his desk.

He fished his water bottle from his backpack and shuffled to the water cooler, patting Denver on the back as he passed by. He turned the corner of the middle row, and there she was.

Books were piled in a corner on her desk. Sudoku and crossword puzzles lay scattered next to her keyboard and mouse. Natalia leaned forward, her pencil jumping around the crossword.

How about a five-letter word for what you are?

Adrian crouched down to fill up his bottle, the dispenser booming as massive bubbles erupted from the base of the five-gallon jug. He shot a glance in Natalia's direction. And as she had done every single day since she started working here, she kept her focus entirely on the papers on her desk.

Before the new year, it had been thick engineering textbooks. She could even bring in her personal laptop, something no one else had ever been allowed to do. They all had school work. Why was she so special to get this privilege?

"I'm writing my thesis," she'd always tell anyone who asked. Apparently, a thesis was all it took to receive this special treatment. All Adrian could do was roll his eyes every time she said this.

Natalia on her high horse. He expected nothing less from someone who went to C.U. When they weren't too busy partying, they surely had their noses pointed in the air. *Probably to smell that fresh Boulder air. Buncha hippies.*

Before he turned away from the water cooler, he sent one more glare in her direction, burning it into the back of her head.

Only a person with no soul could just sit there while someone stares them down.

Adrian rolled his eyes before pivoting around to chat with Melissa at her desk.

Someone who actually gets me.

They had started together four years earlier in the same training class. At opposite ends of their twenties, they had developed an older sister/younger brother type of relationship. She knew everything about his life, and he knew everything about Melissa's sexual escapades, no matter how strongly he begged her to keep those stories to herself.

"Good morning, Adrian!" Melissa greeted.

"Morning." He leaned against the wall separating his row from her desk, planting his elbows on top to have a clear view of Melissa.

"Y'all talking about gambling again?" she asked. "You know Texas Hold'em comes from my state. I should be a natural."

Adrian laughed. "Of course. It's in the name. You *should* be a natural? I take it you're actually not?"

"Ha! My deadbeat dad was a gambling addict. At least that's what Ma tells me. I don't think we so much as had a deck of cards in the house after he left. I've never even been to a casino."

"Really? There's so much more to do at casinos besides gambling. Especially out in Vegas." Adrian drummed his fingers on the ledge above Melissa's desk.

"Look at you. *Days* into being twenty-one and already trying to make me sin. Nice try, bro, but you won't catch me there. I don't care how good the Blue Man Group is. I gotta stand by my principles." Melissa pulled out a book from her purse under the desk and plopped it next to her keyboard.

"Fair enough. What if I had a poker night at my house? Would you at least come?"

"Sure, I'll come to hang out, but I'm not gonna play. Not that I know how."

"Deal. And if you ever change your mind about learning to play, just let me know."

"You know I wouldn't ask anyone else to teach me. We still on for lunch today?" Melissa raised her eyebrows.

"Yeah. I was thinking we'd go grab a slice at Anthony's. What do you think?"

"Let's do it," she said, rubbing her palms together in anticipation. "My favorite place." Melissa's work phone rang, so Adrian returned to his desk.

Denver had struck up a conversation with Natalia in front of him. He was telling her about their upcoming Vegas trip, and she shared stories of the few times she had gone "with her girls" and all the fun they had club-hopping all over the Strip.

Adrian rolled his eyes again. If Natalia didn't hurry and quit—she openly discussed her job hunt in the engineering field—his eyes just might get stuck staring at the back of his skull. Of course she had been to Vegas multiple times before.

She probably walks into clubs, gets free drinks all night, and dances in those little circles with her girlfriends. The kind who shout like emotional teenagers every time "their song" comes on.

Adrian didn't *need* to be liked by others, but he still wondered *why* Natalia treated him the way she did.

Since the first day Natalia had strolled into the offices, she had always given off a sense that she thought the job was beneath her. And what Adrian had come to know after working in the organization for so long was that *everyone* deserved better than their current roles. Even their sheepish manager, Lopez, could have made double the salary had he just ventured out and taken a job with a different company that valued its employees.

What made Natalia so special to flaunt this simple fact around? Speaking of special, why did she get her own set of unique rules in the call center? Cell phones weren't allowed to be used during office hours. Personal use of the internet was strictly forbidden. However, Natalia was approved to bring in her laptop from home to work on her thesis all day. Half the staff in the call center were college students with plenty of homework they could have focused on throughout the day. Yet, none of them were granted these same privileges.

No, Adrian had to find back channel methods just to open an internet browser on his work computer whenever Lopez stepped out of the room, leaving him enough time to simply check his email.

It was unfair. And it infuriated Adrian still to this day.

"Yeah, I'm taking this guy," Denver said, nodding toward Adrian, and snapping him out of his daydream into the past. "Should be a good time with lots of cards."

Natalia still refused to look in his direction, even with her conversation directly involving Adrian.

C'mon, Denver. Why are you telling her about our trip? It's none of her business. We don't need all of her negative energy.

As if she heard his thoughts, Natalia turned her head and looked straight at him. Heat filled his body and flushed his face. She looked like she wanted to reach over the partition and strangle him. So much hate swam behind her eyes.

Fortunately, Adrian's phone rang, and he hurried to answer it.

If she didn't want to waste her precious seconds saying a simple hello, then he wouldn't waste his in return. Two could play whatever game this was, and Adrian was too competitive to lose.

CHAPTER *Three*

NATALIA ENJOYED a relaxing weekend before returning to work the following Monday, the final day of January. She had spent the time sending out more job applications and lounging around in her sweatpants while snow fell outside.

The new work week started off on the right foot. No Adrian in sight.

She expected as much since she knew he had classes on Mondays and Wednesdays, and she counted on those two days as a break from the never-ending mind games. She'd celebrate the occasion of no interruptions by working on a booklet of sudoku puzzles to pass the day.

The desk next to Natalia's was used for the employees who didn't have a set schedule. Most of the time it was empty, especially in the off-season, but today Caroline Smith had taken the spot, her backpack, lunchbox, and a stack of books scattered across the desk.

Caroline was another one of the retirees who worked roughly one day a week at the call center, plus another part-time job for an airline. Free flights and baseball tickets. What else could one need?

"Morning, Natalia," Caroline said. "How have you been?"

Caroline was a tall woman with short, wavy hair, a stern expression usually stuck on her face. Her deep voice was the perfect complement to her no-nonsense approach to life. Many in the call center avoided Caroline, her intensity too much to handle for most. She had once waved her arms at the team's general manager when he visited the call center—an extremely rare occurrence—all to shush him while she was on a phone call.

"Hey, Caroline," Natalia said, swiveling around to face her. "I've been doing pretty good. How about you?"

"Doing great!" A smile touched Caroline's lips. "Just got back from a trip to Arizona. Spent a week there. I like getting away from the cold as much as I can."

"Oh good! What did you do out there?" Natalia shifted forward in her seat to give her full attention.

"Mostly gambling at the casinos. Ended up winning fifteen dollars when it was all said and done, so I can't complain." She clapped her hands together, maintaining a proud grin.

"Fifteen bucks, plus the free drinks, right? That's definitely winning."

Caroline chuckled. "Yes, it is. Do you enjoy going to casinos?"

Natalia bobbed her head side to side. "Yeah. I don't go often, but I always have a fun time. Blackjack is my game."

"Me too. Say, would you be interested in joining me on a trip to Vegas in a couple of weeks? I know it's short notice, so I understand if you can't."

The question caught Natalia off guard. She had become friendly enough with Caroline over the past year, even had lunch with her on several occasions. But now she was proposing a trip together out of the blue. To Las Vegas? Caroline was in her sixties. What exactly did she want to get out of taking a twenty-three-year-old friend to Sin City? *Wasn't Denver just talking about a trip to Vegas last week? Must be something in the air.*

"I'm sorry, when would this be?" Natalia asked, already thinking up which excuse to use.

The first weekend of February was the Super Bowl, and her

family always hosted a big party. The second weekend was Valentine's Day, so she could say that her boyfriend had a romantic weekend planned for them. A total lie, because she was preparing to end things with him at some point this week.

"It would be February fourteenth through the eighteenth. Monday through Friday."

Natalia was expecting a weekend trip, so this made her excuse even easier. "Oh, I don't know if I can afford to do that. I was just off for six weeks. I don't think I'd be able to get another week off approved."

They didn't have paid time off in the call center. If you missed a day, that was your problem. Vacations truly needed to be saved up for, especially for the broke college kids in the office. Natalia had just received her first paycheck in two months because of her extended time off. And while she had minimal expenses, thanks to living at home while she figured out her next move in life, she couldn't exactly pay for a week-long trip to Vegas.

Caroline frowned while she stared at her desk, calculating something in her head.

"Well, your flight will be covered," she said. "We'll fly standby with my buddy passes I get from the airline. The room is already covered with my points I've built up at the hotel. All you'd really need to pay for is your food and entertainment. And as for the time off, I don't see it being a problem. Spring training doesn't start until March, so it's still not going to be all that busy around here."

Natalia no longer had an excuse she could play. In fact, part of her was intrigued by the offer of basically a free trip to Las Vegas. She had enough money to cover food and gambling, and possibly even a show. And it's not like she was trying to move up the corporate ladder at the Rockies, so the idea of asking for another week off didn't seem all that daunting after all. Some of the retirees disappeared for months on end and still kept their positions, dropping in whenever they wanted, as if the call center were a barbershop.

"Can I think about it and let you know by tomorrow?" Natalia asked.

"Absolutely. I'm still going, regardless, and will book the trip this evening. Just let me know and I can add on your buddy pass for the flight if you decide to come."

Natalia nodded. "Will do." Not everyone in the call center was the kindest to Caroline, but Natalia took the time to know her better, rather than jumping to conclusions. This had allowed a personal friendship with Caroline to blossom into a relationship that apparently warranted a trip out of town.

Deep down, Natalia *wanted* to go on the trip, but still needed to convince herself, or rather, justify it.

Will it really be all that fun going with Caroline? Won't she be going to sleep by nine o'clock most nights? That city doesn't even come to life until eleven. But it's a free trip. I guess I'll be single by then. Maybe I can find some guys to flirt with just to shake off the rust before I go back in the dating world.

Natalia would end up spending the next hour talking herself into it. Taking a second vacation so soon after arriving back from an extended trip seemed borderline chaotic, but she would start a new job in the coming months, and there was no saying when her next vacation would actually be. She would need to hit the ground running at whichever engineering firm she ended up with to best position herself for growth.

It might not be the most thrilling of trips to Vegas, but I'll still have a good time.

She got up and filled her water bottle, stopping at the massive corkboard on the wall nearest her desk, where the weekly schedules were posted. Nothing was even up yet for this particular week in question, meaning Lopez hadn't finalized the schedule.

See, another reason to just submit for the time off and see what happens.

She shuffled to the filing cabinet that stored the forms needed to request time off and pulled it open to retrieve a blank sheet.

Here goes nothing. If it gets approved, I'll go. If not, then I won't. Literally nothing I can do about that. This is in Lopez's hands now.

She returned to her desk and filled out the form, sensing Caroline trying to look over her shoulder. The form remained on her desk for the next fifteen minutes while she stared at it, still contemplating any reason she could think of to not go.

"Alright, Caroline," she said, stirring Caroline out of the romance book she had her nose deep into. The TV had been turned on at some point—Natalia hadn't noticed until now—but she didn't care, for the background noise drowned out their conversation from everyone else. "I'm going to submit this request for time off. If he approves it, I'll be joining you."

Caroline smiled, a move that looked somehow out-of-place on her typically emotionless face. "Well, that's great. I look forward to it. I think we'll have a great time. You've been to Vegas before, right?"

"I have. Actually grew up going there every summer. We'd take a road trip to Disneyland each year and always stayed a day in Vegas along the way. I've only gone a couple of times since turning twenty-one, but I'm still very familiar with the Strip and where everything is."

"Perfect. So you'll be okay going out, in case I go to bed early."

Natalia felt like she was being sold on the trip by a master salesperson, overcoming every objection she had, even the ones she hadn't voiced aloud.

"It's been a while since I've been to Vegas as a young, attractive girl," Caroline said. "But do you feel safe enough when you're out there?"

Natalia nodded. "Yeah, I know the places to avoid, especially if I'm walking by myself. I always cut through the hotels when I can. Most of the crazies are out on the Strip."

"Glad to hear. I'm so excited you're doing this. Are you going to hand in your time off request today?"

Natalia picked up the sheet and nodded. "Hopefully he'll

respond today, so you can just book my buddy pass tonight when you do everything else."

Caroline snatched the form from her hand. "I'll get us an answer right now." She stormed into their manager's office before Natalia even realized what was happening.

"Wait," she said, but Caroline was gone.

Natalia swiveled around and peeked over the ledge—where Denver sat—for a view of Lopez's office, Caroline chatting with him as he studied the time off request.

Oh my God, what is this lady doing right now?

Caroline was aggressive in her pursuits, perhaps one of the reasons she rubbed so many of their colleagues the wrong way. But she was simply a woman who knew what she wanted and went after it with all of her might. And after forty years in the workforce, she was hardly intimidated by their skittish manager, Jay Lopez.

She returned less than a minute later with the time-off request signed and approved by Lopez.

"Done," Caroline said, tossing the form and Natalia's desk and returning to her own seat, where she opened her book without another word.

Maybe Vegas will be more interesting than I realize. Does Caroline just go around town pushing people around? Does she shake down blackjack dealers if they go five hands in a row without busting?

Natalia was suddenly giddy with anticipation at the upcoming trip. It wouldn't be the typical drunken nights out with her girlfriends, as she had done in the past. Far from it, but it would have new dynamics. *Different.*

Caroline snapped her book shut and put it down, turning to Natalia. "I forgot to mention one thing. We'll be joining a couple of others on this trip, if you don't mind."

"Oh? Who?" Her stomach sank.

"Denver and Adrian."

A week in Vegas with Adrian? He'll have *to notice me there. Let the games begin.*

CHAPTER *Four*

The next two weeks flew by in a hurry, and Mr. Asshole still didn't speak to Natalia, despite knowing he would soon be in a different city with her, likely sitting across from her at dinner, and spending extended time with her and their senior friends in a setting that couldn't be more different than from call center.

How does he do this?! Natalia had asked herself during those two weeks since agreeing to go on the trip. She heard him speak with Denver about their upcoming plans—she sat right in front of them, after all. Denver mentioned multiple times that Caroline and Natalia would join them on Monday morning, even planning a trip for all four of them to visit the Hoover Dam, since they'd have a rental car at their disposal.

Caroline spoke with Adrian about the trip once too, citing how she and Natalia were really looking forward to it.

Yet, through all that, Adrian still refused to say a single word to Natalia, despite the forty-one trips to the water cooler where he continued with his awkward, narrow stare at his bottle. She had pretended to sneeze while he was at the water cooler—and thought she did a phenomenal job making it sound real—and he still refused to look her direction.

The king of assholes. I hate *that man.*

Natalia and Caroline were set to fly out in two days, but first, they had a day of festivities at work. The second Saturday of February was the annual on-sale day for Rockies tickets. Tickets went on sale for all eighty-one games of the season, and the morning was an absolute blitz on the phones as thousands of fans would call in, mostly to get seats for the home opener in April and the fireworks games in July.

It was the only day of the year when every single call center employee was required to work, forcing the team to split up between the main call center and an overflow office they had up on the third level, suite level. The phones turned on at nine o'clock, and hundreds of callers would remain in queue until noon when things somewhat cooled down.

Despite being the busiest day of the year, the office hummed with excitement. People who rarely worked together had the opportunity to catch up. Baseball was right around the corner, which meant so was the spring and summer. On-sale day was a rare slice of joy for those in the call center, and the only day of the year when both breakfast and lunch were catered.

Today was Natalia's first experience of on-sale day, but all she could think about was another opportunity to get Adrian to speak to her before they wandered around the desert together. She thought the odds might be in her favor, considering she had overheard Denver mention that he and Adrian would leave for the airport immediately after their shift ended today. Vegas would be at the forefront of Adrian's mind. Surely he would clear the tension that had grown so awkward and heavy between them before he left.

Further playing into her hands was the special seating arrangement drawn up for the day. Lopez assigned both Adrian and Natalia to desks on the suite level, and they'd be in the same row, four seats apart.

Once she saw this seating chart posted on Friday, Natalia knew she had to crank up the heat for the big day. She dressed in a form-fitting pencil skirt that cut off just above the knees, revealing the Speedy Gonzales tattoo just above her ankle. She had even shaved—in the winter—to make sure her legs were as appealing as possible.

Natalia also wore a blouse that revealed the slightest glimpse of cleavage. She questioned herself as she dressed earlier this morning, wondering why she was putting in so much effort into her appearance to get Adrian's attention. She hated him, after all.

It's not for Adrian. It's for me. I'm freshly single, going to Vegas in two days, and life is good. I can get sexy all for myself if I want to.

Natalia had indeed dumped her boyfriend last week, an event that required a two-hour discussion over the phone. She had been upset by the breakup, but it wasn't one that knocked her down. In fact, it did quite the opposite. She hadn't realized how much that relationship was dragging her down, and suddenly felt free to plan her days as she pleased.

Now, Natalia only worried about what awaited in the future, mainly her new job as an engineer, whenever those cards fell into place.

When Natalia arrived at work, she headed straight for the main call center, where all the staff was to meet for breakfast and a morning meeting before the phones turned on. The room was crowded, people standing in the rows with nowhere to sit. A group even huddled in the hallway just to have some fresh air.

"Damn, girl," Melissa said when Natalia stepped in, forcing her way to her friend's desk. "Look at you. I know you said you're a model, but my goodness, you're *hot*! Look at those calves. You could kill someone with those things."

"Oh, thanks, girl," Natalia said, grinning from ear to ear.

Melissa sat behind Denver, so Natalia spun around to see him.

"You look very nice, Natalia," he said. "Like you should be the boss around here."

Natalia noticed two suitcases parked on the side of Denver's desk. "Thanks, Denver. You're off to Vegas today, right?"

"Yep," Denver replied, patting the closest suitcase. "These are mine and Adrian's bags. We're off as soon as Lopez says we can leave. We're still on for Monday at the Hoover Dam?"

"Of course."

What Natalia wanted to say was that Denver should tell his little buddy to stop being such a prick if they all wanted to have a fun vacation. But she could never be so aggressive toward Denver. He was the ultimate gentleman, raised with every manner in the book, humbled by growing up during segregation. That Denver was close friends with Adrian was perhaps the only reason she held out hope for Mr. Asshole at all. Denver was a sound judge of character, and would never suggest spending an entire week in Las Vegas with someone he didn't trust. Their solid friendship was Adrian's only redeeming quality.

She spotted Adrian on the other side of the room, chatting with a guy named Michael, who somehow worked only four times a year.

Natalia hadn't paid any attention when she entered the room, but was now realizing that several of the men in the office were trying to steal a quick glance, mainly looking at her legs, validating that she had accomplished what she set out for.

Lopez called for silence in the room and delivered his version of a motivational speech. He stressed the usual topics of getting on and off each call promptly without making the customer feel rushed, plus the opportunity for upselling. There was no better chance than on-sale day to encourage fans to spend big money on their purchase, especially after they waited on hold for an hour—they wanted to get their time's worth of tickets. After concluding with an offer of support should anyone need it throughout the day, the meeting adjourned and everyone went their separate ways to their desks.

Natalia wished Melissa and Denver a good day before slipping out to the hallway and to the crowded elevator lobby where the upstairs crew was waiting. Sixteen of them in total crammed into one elevator, Natalia ending up smashed next to Adrian. She felt his elbow rubbing against her arm as they rode up one level. He looked over at her and smiled, saying, "Morning."

Her heart hammered against her chest. The moment had finally arrived, and it had come so far out of the blue that she nearly forgot how to respond like a normal human being.

"Hey… good morning," she replied, immediately pissed at herself for missing the opportunity to start an actual conversation.

He knows I exist, she thought as the elevator doors parted on the third floor and everyone piled out, Adrian immediately hurrying to get three paces ahead of Natalia. *He made contact with me, even if he didn't want to. But he knows I'm here. And he didn't just say good morning, he* smiled *at me.*

Maybe everyone had been right about Adrian taking his time to open up to people. Nine months in and he finally said hello. Maybe in another six he would ask how she was doing.

He just knows you're going to Vegas together and is running out of time to keep up this shunning. It has nothing to do with the outfit or how close we just stood next to each other. He just doesn't want to ruin the trip.

And if that was the only reason he'd speak to Natalia, then so be it. A memorable trip was truly the only objective that mattered.

But she couldn't resist the excitement that accompanied that first spoken word from Adrian's mouth. He *was* capable of speaking to her. *Acknowledging* her. Not only did it change the dynamic for their trip—she was counting on at least a full day of the continued antics—it changed everything for the rest of their time working together. The thrill was gone. The game was over. What would Natalia worry about during the slow days, now that Mr. Asshole had finally admitted she existed in the same world as him?

The mind games had become such a part of her life during the past couple of months that she felt even more freedom on top of being newly single. She really was heading into this Vegas trip on top of the world, and nothing could bring her down. Not even

Adrian, who she figured she'd end up stuck with alone once Denver and Caroline both called it an early night.

Adrian didn't matter, though. Not in Vegas, not ever. She would lay out some ground rules once they were there and make sure he understood to stay out of her way if she wanted to strike up a conversation with a man.

The upcoming trip was her opportunity to find herself. Some time away, on her own, was exactly what she needed to figure out who she wanted to be in this next phase of her life.

For now, she had to get through the busy day ahead. Just before the phones came to life, she glanced over and caught Adrian gazing at her legs.

CHAPTER *Five*

I CAN'T BELIEVE *I actually have to talk to her today,* Adrian thought when he woke up on Monday morning. The sun beamed into his hotel room, forcing its way through the thin curtain hanging over the window. Adrian swung his legs out of bed and flung the curtain all the way open to enjoy a scenic view of behind the Las Vegas Strip. The MGM Grand, Tropicana, and Planet Hollywood were all within his immediate view.

Saturday and Sunday had been a blur. When they had arrived Saturday evening, they checked in at the hotel before heading out to dinner. Being such a long day that started with working in a different time zone, they were both tired after dinner. Denver went to bed, promising a busier day on Sunday once he had more energy.

Adrian, energized by Las Vegas and all of its lights, stayed up until midnight at a five-dollar blackjack table where he broke even while sipping on rum and Cokes throughout the night. A success in his book.

Sunday wasn't busy by any means, but definitely more fun. Pro basketball games started at 10 A.M. local time, so he and Denver grabbed a couple seats in the Bellagio Sports Book, bet one hundred dollars each on the Los Angeles Lakers to cover a three-point spread over the Phoenix Suns, and enjoyed a fresh drink every half hour while they watched the game.

By the end of the game, they'd each had six drinks, the Lakers had covered, and they stumbled to the counter to collect their winnings.

"Hundred bucks to start the trip," Denver said. "Not bad."

Since they were drunk, they ended up lost on their way to find the In-N-Out Burger, somehow needing to cross the interstate to reach it—which they did.

The alcohol had worn them down too much to play in a poker tournament. They needed sharp minds if they wanted any chance of lasting to actually win money. So they spent the rest of the afternoon hopping from casino to casino and playing different table games.

Even without having played a poker tournament, the first two days had been perfect. Monday morning, however, the dynamic of the trip was about to change for good.

Natalia and Caroline were flying in, and they would all head to the Hoover Dam for a day of sightseeing.

So far, Adrian hadn't spent a penny on this trip. He had no room to complain, but why on Earth did Denver have to invite Caroline?

Caroline wasn't even the problem. He had no issues with her directly and believed the three of them would've had a great time. But Caroline invited Natalia along, and now the entire trip was spiraling out of control. How could Adrian enjoy himself if the most miserable person he knew would be there every step of the way?

She'll probably complain about the drinks not being strong enough, or the food not being good enough.

Adrian was cornered. He was a night owl and would stay out until at least two if the night warranted. Denver had yet to stay up past ten o'clock, and he imagined Caroline would be no different. So who would be left from their group to spend that time with?

He rolled his eyes for the first of what he expected to be hundreds of times over the upcoming week.

Maybe I can find a late tournament to play every night. That gives me a valid and totally reasonable excuse to go off on my own.

"Ready?" Denver asked, sipping a cup of coffee he had made, patting Adrian on the back as they gathered in the kitchen of their hotel suite.

"Sure." Adrian's stomach swirled in angst. The moment he was dreading kept drawing nearer.

He followed Denver outside, where they waited on the curb. Caroline had rented a car and would stop by to pick them up.

I'll probably sit in the back seat with Natalia, who has never spoken to me. How fun!

"So, Denver," Adrian said. "How did this all come to be? With Caroline and Natalia joining us."

"Oh, wasn't much." Denver took a sip of his coffee. "I was just telling Caroline about the trip. She works for Frontier, you know, and always has free flights. I told her to come along if she was available, and apparently she was. I think she invited Natalia a couple weeks after that, since you were going to be here."

"I see. Did she not know that Natalia *hates* me?"

"Hate? That's a strong word." Denver chuckled, crumpling up his now empty coffee cup.

"You're right. It's more like she *loathes* me."

Denver laughed to himself. "I don't think that's true, or else she wouldn't have agreed to come on the trip."

"I don't know," Adrian said, shaking his head as he stared at the Strip in the distance. "We've never spoken to each other. Since the day she started last summer, I can count the words we've exchanged on one hand."

"I'm sure you're being dramatic. You two sit less than six feet apart."

"Exactly, and have you ever seen us having a conversation? When I fill up my water, she won't even look in my direction."

"Maybe she likes you."

Now was Adrian's turn to laugh. "Good one, Denver. I'm sure that's exactly it. She likes me and agreed to this trip to finally make her move. Maybe we'll fall in love and get married at one of these chapels."

Denver shrugged. "Crazier things have happened. Especially here."

Adrian didn't appreciate the serious tone of his friend. Denver had proven plenty wise over their time working together. He had seen everything during his six decades in this world and never hesitated to share his insights.

Surely the situation with Natalia wasn't a crush—she seemed much too intense to play such childish games. But the idea opened Adrian's mind to the possibility that it wasn't necessarily hatred. To be fair, he didn't speak to her, either. But that was just because she didn't seem to want to be spoken to. At least by him.

"What do you even know about Natalia?" Adrian asked, hoping for anything he could use as a weapon during this trip. It was inevitable they would clash at some point.

"Not a ton. She's a sweet girl. Very smart. I know she speaks Spanish, and just got back from a trip to Colombia to visit her family."

Adrian rolled his eyes, and Natalia wasn't even here yet. All he overheard during the past few weeks was Natalia telling everyone about her big family trip to South America. She really lived the high life, apparently.

"I think you two will get along just fine," Denver continued. "Maybe you just need a trip like this to be forced to spend time together to understand each other a little better."

But I don't want *to understand Natalia. If I wanted that, I would've already tried.*

Adrian's desires would have to join him in the backseat.

"They're here," Denver said, nodding to the car pulling up to the curb with the hazards flashing.

Caroline was driving, and Natalia was already in the back seat, sitting behind the driver's seat.

Adrian pulled open the door, knots twisting in his stomach as he sat down next to Natalia.

CHAPTER *Six*

MONDAY HAPPENED to be Valentine's Day, and the day started bright and early for Natalia as she headed to the airport to meet Caroline for their flight. She looked forward to leaving the cold weather behind. Vegas wouldn't be its scorching summer self, but would be plenty warmer than what they'd been dealing with in Colorado.

Natalia had grown eager to close the book on her ex-boyfriend with the help of this trip. She hadn't realized it until arriving at the airport, but a new chapter awaited. It had been years since she'd gone to Vegas as a single woman, and she was more than ready to cut loose. Maybe she'd find a guy to spend the evenings with and forget all about the misery she was leaving at home.

These thoughts motivated Natalia throughout her breakfast with Caroline in the terminal. It wasn't until they landed in Vegas three hours later that she started to grow anxious about the prospect of spending the next five days with Adrian. They had a group trip planned with Denver and Adrian to visit the Hoover Dam upon their arrival, followed by five days of wandering the Strip.

Five days.

Of silence? Awkwardness? Perhaps regular conversation?

She didn't know what to expect, and that troubled her mind. Just because he had finally spoken to her in the elevator at work didn't mean things would magically be different with her arrival.

This was very much Adrian's trip to Vegas, considering it was Denver's gift to him for his twenty-first birthday last month. While they hadn't explicitly agreed to hang out with Adrian and Denver during the week, it was inevitable, since Caroline had made the plans for this trip based on everything Denver had booked. They were even staying at the same hotel one block off the Strip, and Caroline volunteered her rental car for use whenever anyone needed it.

"You have a good nap?" Caroline asked once they prepared to get off the plane.

"Yes, ready for a fun week now."

"We just gotta get our bags and the car, and we'll be on our way."

"How long of a drive is it to the dam?" Natalia asked, wanting to know how much time she had to prepare for Mr. Asshole.

"About forty-five minutes."

Natalia felt her stomach sink. She was about to be stuck in a car with Adrian for a ninety-minute round trip. Ninety minutes of pure torture.

He broke the ice at work. Now I'll talk to him. Force the conversation.

She didn't have time for games now that they had arrived. She was here for a fun week of drinking, dancing, and walking the Strip.

After picking up their luggage, they rode the train to the car rental offices, where Caroline had a VIP pass to skip the long lines. It was maybe the fastest Natalia had ever gone through such a line, and they were on the road in just ten minutes.

"Maybe you should sit in the back with Adrian so that Denver can ride in the front more comfortably," Caroline said after they loaded their suitcases into the trunk.

"Of course," Natalia replied. *Why shouldn't I be stuck in the back with Mr. Asshole?*

Caroline didn't need directions as she was a natural in the city.

"So, Caroline," Natalia said, sitting behind her. "What do you know about Adrian? I've worked with him for about nine months now and know nothing about the guy."

"He's a good guy," Caroline said. "I know he's very passionate about working in baseball, hopes to make a career out of it. Let's see. He's finishing college. Has a girlfriend he's been with for a while. Been with the Rockies for four years now. And I know he loves to play poker. Outside of that, I guess I don't know much else about him."

"I see. I've never had the chance to really speak to him."

"Well, I'm sure you two will have plenty of time to get to know each other on this trip."

"I look forward to it."

Natalia didn't, but she had to seem cordial, at least in her appearances with Adrian in front of Denver and Caroline. If he could go nine months of playing mind games, she could do the same for a week. She could keep a fake smile on her face while the four of them were hanging out, but when the time came for her and Adrian to be alone, she could tell him off and leave him behind.

I can't actually be that mean, can I?

She didn't *need* to be with Adrian just because the two older folks they traveled with wanted to go to bed early. If he hadn't been so stuck up for the last nine months, then maybe she would consider spending more time with him, but she owed him nothing. And she refused to become his tour guide for his first trip to Vegas.

I'm going to find a man I can have fun with while I'm out here. Adrian has a girlfriend, so that's his problem if he can't do the same. All I can do is be upfront and tell him what I'm planning to do on this trip.

"We should have a good time," Caroline said. "I know Denver loves to play poker, too, as do I. They'll probably spend a lot of time playing in tournaments, but I'd rather spend a day at the blackjack tables."

"I'll be right there with you."

Natalia wouldn't dare leave Caroline on this trip, especially since she was paying for everything. Whatever Caroline wanted to do, Natalia would do. Her free time would come at night, as long as she could shake free of Adrian.

You're overreacting. He obviously doesn't want to spend time with you, either, or else he would have spoken with you about making plans for the trip. If he has a girlfriend, why isn't she on this trip with him? Maybe Denver said this was a guy's trip, then changed all of that when Caroline inquired.

They arrived at the hotel ten minutes later, Caroline pointing to different hotels to share stories of times she had stayed, won, or lost at each one. She had tabs on every building on and off the Strip, and knew exactly where to find the cheapest food, drinks, and gambling.

Natalia had been too distracted with scheming up different ways to get rid of Adrian, that she didn't realize the opportunity right in front of her. She hadn't set out to become lifelong friends with Caroline, but after traveling together, wouldn't the dynamic of their relationship change? They certainly wouldn't go back to the office and everything would be the same. Perhaps their friendship would strengthen, and they would go on trips again in the future. Or maybe Caroline would lose interest in Natalia once she realized she didn't actually want to spend an *entire* day at a blackjack table. Natalia wanted to see shows, go out to a nice dinner, and ride out a good buzz with one of those tall frozen drinks while she roamed the Strip. And nightclubs.

Natalia was a rare breed in her high school days, befriending people from all walks of life. She played on the basketball team, joined the color guard, and always kept her grades up. She hung out with jocks, the band, nerds, and the outcasts. This resulted in her having a wide range of friends, and this same approach carried through her college years, too.

She knew multiple people with connections in Las Vegas. Club promoters, bartenders, ticket vendors. She never had to pay to get into a club, and once inside of one, never had to spend money on drinks. With a quick text message, Natalia could have a list of night clubs she could enter at her will tonight, and every night for the rest of the week. Maybe she'd invite Adrian for one night out.

"There they are," Caroline said, pulling into the hotel's roundabout in front of the entrance.

Natalia looked up and saw Adrian and Denver standing on the curb, dressed in jeans and windbreakers.

Caroline pulled up to them, Denver waving with a wide grin before opening his doors.

"Hey, Caroline," he said. "Natalia. Good to see you guys. Everything go good with the flight?"

"Sure did," Caroline said.

Natalia kept her stare on Denver while Adrian opened his door and sat down, an entire two feet across from her.

She looked at him, keeping a stern expression, and said, "Hey."

"Hello," Adrian replied, buckling his seat belt, his voice more chipper than she expected.

There we go. We each spoke to each other. Now we can go back to our corners and pretend it never happened.

"Thanks for driving, Caroline," Adrian said.

"My pleasure," she replied, taking off in search of the freeway.

Oh, now he's polite?

Natalia pulled out her cellphone and scrolled through her Facebook feed. That would at least help from feeling *too* awkward in the backseat. She sent messages to her friends who worked in Vegas, making plans for the night ahead.

Caroline and Denver carried on with their own conversation, and Adrian gazed out his window.

Is he thinking about the best ways to not talk to me? Let's make him uncomfortable.

Natalia reached into her purse and pulled out three Valentine's cards and three mini packets of M&M's.

"I got everyone a little Valentine's Day treat," she said,

handing two cards to Denver. "If you can give the extra to Caroline, please."

"I'll give her the card. I'm keeping the candy."

Everyone laughed.

The cards were the kind kids exchanged in elementary school. Silly images with cheesy quotes. The one she saved for Adrian had an image of a donkey smiling and winking, pointing its hoof to the recipient. "Hee-Haaaaa! Happy Valentine's Day!" was written above the donkey.

The ass for Mr. Asshole, she had thought when she filled out the names on the cards.

"Here you go," she said, handing the Valentine and candy over to Adrian.

"Oh, thank you," he said, grabbing the gifts. "You didn't need to. That's so nice of you."

Three whole sentences. Wow! Maybe he is *human.*

"You're welcome. I figured everyone should get a Valentine on Valentine's Day."

"Well, I'm sorry I didn't bring you anything. Maybe I can buy you a drink later?" Adrian held his stare on Natalia. His eyes were much softer without the usual look of disdain.

Natalia paused. The conversation was going a little too normal, as if there hadn't been a ton of tension in their past that was suddenly being brushed aside in the name of common courtesy.

Appearances, Natalia, she reminded herself. *Make it all look good. Clearly he is. Maybe you can take his drink later and throw it in his face. But for now, make it look good.*

"That would be great," she said. "Thank you."

As if dealing with Adrian wasn't enough, Denver made things worse.

"Left your girlfriend behind on Valentine's Day," he said to Adrian. "To come to Vegas with another woman. Was she okay with that?"

Denver chuckled at himself. Adrian flushed red, something only Natalia had seen.

He gulped before replying. "Yes, she's fine with it. We had our Valentine's celebration on Friday night."

"Of course you did," Denver said. "You're one of the good ones. And I'm sure you'll be taking her back a nice present, too."

"Exactly. It's all figured out."

Denver looked over his shoulder at Natalia. "And what about you? Did you leave a boyfriend back at home today, too?"

She could feel Adrian staring at her out of the corner of her eye. Why did he suddenly have an interest in this answer? Couldn't he have asked her about her relationship status any time during the last nine months?

"No boyfriend," Natalia said. "I actually just got out of a relationship."

"Nice," Denver said. "I mean, I'm sorry."

Natalia laughed. "It's okay. It's for the better."

"Okay then. Nice." Denver laughed. "Single in Vegas. I remember those days. Don't go too crazy this week."

Now was Natalia's turn to blush, but Adrian had already looked back out his window. Melissa had informed Natalia that Adrian might seem disinterested and not engaged in the conversation, but he was always listening. Observing.

Natalia didn't want to give him the chance to be the silent observer. He had spoken, and this opened the door for her to get payback for all the discomfort he had caused her over the past several months.

"So Adrian," she said. "Is your girlfriend that blonde girl I've seen in the call center a couple of times?"

"Yes," he said. His leg started bouncing.

"What's her name?"

"Barbara."

"I see. How are things going with her?" Natalia made a conscious effort to keep her tone light, not wanting to sound like an interrogator.

She couldn't care any less about the answers to these questions, but the more she watched Adrian's leg bounce out of control, the more satisfaction she felt, and the stronger her desire became to keep the questioning going. As far as Denver and Caroline were concerned, they were just getting to know each other in the backseat.

"Things are great. Next month will be five years we've been together. High school sweethearts. Even survived a whole year apart when she went to college in Grand Junction."

"Good for you guys."

"You just broke up with someone?" Adrian asked, flipping the script on Natalia. She had expected to remain in control of the conversation. If Adrian was supposedly so quiet and kept to himself, surely he wouldn't respond with questions of his own. He had just caught her off guard. His leg stopped bouncing.

This asshole knows exactly what he's doing. The mind games continue.

"Yes, we just broke up last week. He's a Marine, so we've done the long-distance thing, too. It's not easy. Good for you for making it through."

"You deserve better," Denver said, turning to look over his shoulder. "I doubt this is the city you'll find better, but who knows?"

Denver's comment ended the conversation in the backseat, Natalia suddenly grateful. She needed to reassess her approach to Adrian. His silence and shunning had long been a mind game, and now it seemed his words also had their own meaning. Melissa had warned her against backing Adrian into a corner. It would make him shut down if he couldn't find a way out.

And he did. Even with the reversal of the conversation, Adrian remained silent as he stared out the window for the next forty minutes while they drove, occasionally responding to something Denver said, but never looking in Natalia's direction. That was more of what she had been expecting.

When they finally arrived at the Hoover Dam, Caroline parked at one of the main observation decks on the side of the road. They had all agreed to not spend the money on tour tickets that would take them deep into the dam. Seeing it was good enough, especially for Adrian and Natalia, who had never been before.

They moved to the rail overlooking the dam for a breathtaking view. The crisp, teal water sat hundreds of feet below, splitting the small mountains to resemble a river. A bridge connected the two sides high above.

Natalia had never felt so small in the world. A breeze blew through, providing waves of white noise, followed by an eerie silence while all four of them gawked into the distance. As an engineer, Natalia had studied plenty about the Hoover Dam throughout school, but seeing it in person validated her career path. Almost a century ago, a team of engineers had gathered to plan and build what would become the largest dam in the United States. This dam resulted in a power plant that fed into the three surrounding states. Those engineers made a difference, made the world a better place. And that's all Natalia wanted to do.

"Let's take a picture," Natalia said, realizing too late that only Adrian was still standing within her proximity. Denver and Caroline had wandered further down the observation deck for a different angle.

Natalia immediately clenched her fists, hoping for some longshot that he hadn't heard her.

That wasn't the case.

Now Adrian thought she was asking him, specifically, to take a picture with her. She couldn't take back her words and would have to power through.

"Okay," he said, sounding unsure if he had understood correctly.

He shuffled next to her, hands stuffed into his jacket's front pockets.

He doesn't want to make contact.

Natalia leaned in closer to him so that their shoulders would touch, and held up her phone to take a picture of the two of them.

The awkward moment passed, the sun right in their faces as they squinted toward the phone to capture a moment Natalia wondered if she could ever make sense of. If you had asked her last week about the odds of being in a photo with Adrian Gonzalez, she would have said there were better chances of an elephant flying from the zoo to take a swim in the Hoover Dam.

But there it was. Proof of a trip with the man she despised. And they were both smiling. It actually looked like they were getting along.

CHAPTER
Seven

THROUGHOUT THE REST of the day, nothing felt quite normal. Despite the Valentine's card, the shared picture, and even some light chatter during their drive back, the tension remained heavy between Adrian and Natalia.

They had stopped in Boulder City for lunch and table games for an hour before returning to their hotel. Less than ten words were exchanged between the two.

They all agreed to have dinner at a buffet, and they settled on the Luxor, per Natalia's recommendation.

Dinner went smoothly. Natalia sat diagonal from Adrian, keeping their direct conversation to a minimum. She still hated the guy. How could he sit there so smugly, yet go about his business as if everything was completely normal? Why couldn't he just speak to her like everyone else he encountered in life? Were there other people who received this spiteful treatment, or was she the only member of an exclusive club?

Natalia had plenty of people who had hated her in high school and college—a natural occurrence for not conforming to the bubbles society had carved out for who she was *supposed* to hang out with.

Yet, she didn't get the sense that Adrian actually hated her. Far from it. It was more like a strong disinterest. She had been so blinded by her own hate to have ever noticed.

His attention had been out the window or on his phone during the excruciating round trip to the Hoover Dam. He made no attempt at small talk with his backseat neighbor.

It was as if her mere existence provided him no value in his odd little life. She could drop dead on the dinner table and he wouldn't even notice, because it changed nothing for his daily operations. He'd probably still go to his poker tournament in the morning as if nothing had happened.

Part of her *wanted* him to hate her. That she knew how to deal with. She could counter his hate with her own, and the mind games could continue. This realization that Adrian didn't actually hate her caused a sinking pit in her stomach. If that was true, then she had wasted time over the past few months. There was no mind game if she was the only who had shown up to play. She had made something out of literally nothing. Adrian wasn't playing games. He had no agenda. He just went about his business, and his business included nothing with Natalia.

After dinner, the dreadful moment had arrived. Even though she knew it was coming, the prospect flattened her spirits, especially after her newfound realizations.

"I'm going to call it a night," Denver said when they finished eating. It was only eight o'clock.

"Me too," Caroline said. "It's been a long day. I'm beat."

The truth was, Natalia could go to bed, too. But she couldn't roll over, not in front of Adrian. What twenty-three-year-old would fly into Vegas and go to bed at eight?

"Are you two going to stay out?" Denver asked, eyebrows raised.

Adrian looked at her from across the table, trying to read her thoughts. It almost looked like he was inviting her to spend the rest of the evening with him.

"I'd like to," Adrian said, his tone suggesting to Natalia to decide.

She rolled up her sleeve and checked her watch, trying to sell her own disinterest. "Okay. I'll go out for a bit. I was up early, so don't want to stay out too late."

"Fair," Adrian said.

"Great, well, we'll let you two get to it," Caroline said, standing up from the table. "Are you good walking back to the hotel later tonight, or do you want to come with us so you can take the car back out?"

"I'm fine walking back, if you are, Natalia," Adrian said in perhaps his most endearing tone so far. He sounded normal, not like Mr. Asshole.

"Yeah, I'm fine with that," she replied.

"That settles it," Caroline said. "Ready to head out, Denver?"

"Ready for a nightcap in the bathtub," Denver said, earning a round of laughter.

"It's his nightly ritual," Adrian added.

"We'll see you two in the morning," Caroline said, pushing in her chair and throwing down a couple of singles for a tip. "And we can plan out the day."

Caroline and Denver left the buffet, Adrian and Natalia breaking away as they walked through the Luxor casino.

"So," Natalia said. "Anything you want to do?"

"Actually, I'd love to get one of those big frozen drinks I see everyone else with. I've only been having drinks in the casinos, and they don't just give those away. Do you want one? I owe you a drink… for Valentine's."

Natalia raised her eyebrows in surprise. She didn't expect Adrian to keep his word regarding the drink. "Sure. Those take a couple hours to finish. We can each have one, then maybe head back?"

Adrian nodded. "Sounds like a plan."

In Vegas, it wasn't hard to find a drink, and they had their frozen yardstick-sized containers filled with piña colada within the next ten minutes.

"So tell me about yourself," Adrian said.

He was loosening up. Natalia sensed it. She no longer felt the disinterest radiating from him. He was speaking *to* her and listening to her responses. He even made eye contact. Were his eyes always so green?

This must be what Melissa was talking about. He's finally feeling comfortable around me and is opening up.

"What do you mean?" Natalia asked, smiling at the anticipation of having an actual adult conversation with Mr. Asshole.

"I know nothing about you. Your name is Natalia Ayala. You recently got back from a long vacation in Colombia. That's about all I know." He let out a nervous laugh. "Tell me about your life. Your family. What do you want to do? Are you looking for a career in sports?"

So you noticed I was gone. And even know where I was. You have been paying attention. The observer.

"Well, you got those two things right, so good job. I'm twenty-three, just graduated in December with my master's in structural engineering from C.U. So no, I don't want a future in sports. My aunt works for the Rockies and helped me get a job that would be good while I worked on my thesis. And I'd say it all worked out. Now I'm looking for work in my field."

"Wow," Adrian said. "A structural engineer? I don't even know what that means."

He laughed at himself, the most innocent sound she had ever heard him make. Not the sound of an asshole.

"What about you?" Natalia asked, taking a long sip from her drink.

"Ah! Not so fast," he said, whipping out his finger and pointing at her. "You haven't told me about your family."

"My bad. I'm the oldest of three. My sister is the middle child —and yes, she acts like it. And my brother is the baby—and yes, he acts like it." They both shared a laugh. "My mom is from Colombia, my dad is from Venezuela, and so much of our family lives here—well, in Colorado. We're all very close with each other."

"That's awesome." A soft smile touched the corners of his mouth.

"Yeah, it's a lot of fun. Okay, now your turn for real."

Natalia found herself consumed by the conversation. She genuinely wanted to know all about Adrian. It was like she had an exclusive VIP pass to learn about his life, something very few could say. They were a little over a quarter of the way finished with their drinks by the time they stepped out, crossing the bridge over to the MGM Grand. Adrian had asked if they could walk on that side of the Strip, since Denver had only wanted to spend time at Bellagio and Caesar's Palace.

"Okay," Adrian said. "I'm also the oldest. Just one little sister. Five years younger. Most of my family is also in the Denver area, with some in New Mexico. My mom and dad are divorced. They split during my junior year of high school, and that's been a lot to deal with. I feel terrible for moving out so soon after I graduated high school and leaving my sister to deal with that on her own. But I had been wanting to live on my own for the longest time."

"I'm so sorry you had to go through that." She saw the tears well in his eyes and felt helpless.

"It's fine. Everyone has moved on with their lives by now. We're good. I still have all of my grandparents, and they all live within five minutes of my mom's house, so it's been easy to stay close. My grandma was recently diagnosed with cancer." Adrian paused and took a long drink. "It's really hard. I don't even know how to explain."

His voice cracked. The surge of emotions had come on much too quickly. Natalia sure didn't see it escalating so fast, so she reached out a hand and rubbed Adrian's shoulder. The contact surprised them both and snapped her back to the reality that they were slowly getting tipsy while walking down the Las Vegas Strip.

"It'll be fine," she said. "Sorry you felt the need to bring it up."

"No, don't be sorry. It's my own fault. I bottle things up and never let them out. Naturally, I'm going to confess all of this to a complete stranger."

Natalia laughed. "Stranger? We've worked together for nine months. It's not like I'm that guy over there."

Natalia pointed to a man dancing on a nearby set of escalators, a beer can in each hand as he belted out the lyrics to Katy Perry's "California Gurls."

Adrian cackled to himself, shaking his head. "No, you're certainly not that guy."

The mood had shifted. Adrian was an open book and Natalia wanted to flip to the pages that explained everything that had puzzled her since last summer. "Can I ask you something?"

"This isn't some weird question about my childhood, is it?"

"No." She chuckled and brushed back her wind-blown hair.

"Okay then, go ahead."

"Why have you never spoken to me until this trip? I've worked at the Rockies since June, and you've never said a word to me." The question was out now, hanging in the air like a piñata waiting to get battered by sugar-crazed children.

Adrian took a drink and kept the straw in his mouth while he stared ahead, obviously searching for an excuse that could sound the slightest bit legitimate. "That can't be true. I've had to have said *something* to you."

"Nothing that I recall. I thought it was strange. We're the only two brown people in the call center. I thought that would count for something. Is it something that I said or did? I just want to know." She didn't want to seem too eager, so she sucked on her straw as if she had only asked his favorite color instead.

Natalia didn't *want* to know. She *needed* to know. His answer could change the course of whatever messed up relationship they had developed in one short day.

Adrian took a long pause while he sipped his drink. They had passed the strip mall and were now walking in front of the Paris Hotel. Natalia wondered if he would actually blow off the question and soon change the subject.

After a minute, Adrian finally replied, shaking his head with the sorrowful expression one might give when being told a loved one had passed. "I'm so sorry. I don't know what else to say. It's not really my way to introduce myself to new people—that's not something I've ever been comfortable with. That's hardly an excuse. You must think I'm such an asshole."

Mr. Asshole, to be correct.

"I don't know," he continued. "I figured you didn't want to speak to me, either, since you never did. See, I don't expect people to introduce themselves to me since I don't do the same. I guess that left us in a position of just not speaking to each other. It might sound crazy, but I've had lots of coworkers at past jobs who came and went without ever speaking a word. Kind of how the full-timers treat us at the Rockies. I don't take it personally. Some people show up to work to get the job done and leave. Not everyone is interested in socializing and making friends, so I figured that was you. You would come in and always had your face buried in a book or your school work. I guess that's on me for making assumptions."

"Wow," Natalia said, her pillars of hatred suddenly wobbly. "So this whole time you haven't spoken to me because you assumed I was focused on other things. I *was,* don't get me wrong, but I wouldn't have been offended if you just said hello during one of your hundred trips to the water cooler."

Adrian busted out laughing. They sounded like old friends catching up, not two people just getting to know each other.

"I don't mean to laugh. It's just crazy to think how much you've noticed me all this time when I thought you were off in your own world, having no interest in talking to me."

"Dude, I sit *right next* to the water cooler. I notice everyone and their drinking habits."

They passed in front of Bally's, drinks half gone, a strong buzz settling in that made Natalia feel alive and ready to party.

"So now that we've cleared the air," Adrian said. "We can talk to each other at work, right?"

Natalia couldn't help but feel the persona of Mr. Asshole fading away, making room for the version of Adrian that everyone else seemed to enjoy. But she didn't want to cave so soon. It would take more than one night of tipsy conversation to erase *months* of hatred. How would he be in the morning once they were sober? Would he resort back to his silent ways, or was he serious about being cordial with Natalia?

They passed the Flamingo, where a group of three showgirls walked up and down the sidewalk outside, Adrian checking all of them out.

"Hey, don't you have a girlfriend?" Natalia asked, smacking him playfully on the arm. "Why are you looking at them?"

Adrian looked at the ground. "Yeah, about that."

"Uh oh. What is it?" She recognized the tone of dread all too well.

"Things aren't going so great right now. In fact, I'm probably going to call it off soon. Maybe when I get back home."

"Wow," Natalia said, eyes wide from the shocking news. "Does she feel the same?"

Adrian shrugged. "It's hard for me to tell. She *seems* happy still, but so do I. Deep down, I'm not. It feels like we're just going through the motions of being in a relationship. Everything has become so routine. I know it sounds cheesy, but it's like the spark is gone. We're basically best friends who hang out all the time. The passion is missing."

"Have you tried anything to bring back that spark?"

"Of course. I've planned date nights. Flowers. Deep conversations. I don't know how to explain it. The love is there, it's just missing something I'm afraid won't come back. She turned twenty-one in September, and I did last month. I think turning that age changes things. More of the world opens up to you at that point, and you learn different things about yourself. We both want something different from our lives. I hope it can be a cordial breakup. I have no ill will towards her. We've just changed since we started dating when we were sixteen. And there's nothing wrong with that."

They passed in front of The Linq and Harrah's.

"That's incredible," Natalia said. "I can't imagine staying with any boyfriend from high school. Seems like a good way to hold you back in college."

Adrian pursed his lips for a moment before speaking. "Maybe so, but I have no regrets. Sure, there were a couple girls I met in college who I would've dated if I was single, but I've never felt like I was missing out on anything. Maybe I'm a sucker for relationships, but I've just never had that desire to date as many girls as I can."

"Well, that's rare," Natalia said with a laugh. "But I'm sorry you're going through this. I hope you don't get *too* hurt. Five years is a long relationship, especially out of high school."

"I'll be okay. Been wrestling with this for the past couple of months now. I think I'm most scared of being single again. I haven't dated someone new in five years—gone through basically my last year of high school and all four years of college without meeting new women. I don't even know what I'm supposed to do. I don't want to meet someone at a bar or a dating app, so where exactly am I supposed to go?"

"You're too worried." She placed a caring hand on his shoulder. "Don't force anything. Just go about your life and be aware of the opportunities that open up to you. I think the harder you try, the more difficult it is. Go out with friends when they invite you. Go on trips by yourself. There are people everywhere. Maybe you can even start talking to one of those girls from your school."

"Good point. And what about you and your Marine? What happened there?"

Natalia rolled her eyes. "It's nothing like your story. We've been on and off for a couple of years, and I decided it's time to just move on. Nothing is coming out of that relationship. I'm not too bothered by the breakup, and neither was he. He still texted me today to say Happy Valentine's Day, and I'm sure he'll try to stay in touch over the next few months, but I'm going to let that fizzle."

"Well, I'm sorry. Breakups suck, even when it's what you want." Adrian stuck out his hand and placed it on Natalia's shoulder to return the favor. The contact sent a confusing flutter through her stomach.

"It really is fine. I'm single. I'm in Vegas. And I'm looking for someone tall, dark, and handsome. So if I find that man, don't be offended when I blow you off for him."

Adrian laughed, returning his hand to his side. "You definitely know what you want. I can respect that. And that's totally fine if you need to go have some time to get your freak on. I'll find something to play."

Natalia howled with laughter. "Get my freak on?! You're too much!"

Adrian smiled. "I don't mean to change the subject, but do you mind if we sit down for like five minutes? We've walked *so* far." He held up his cup, only a quarter full. "And our drinks are almost gone. I'm in that phase where I can't feel my lips."

They shared a laugh as they looked around, not having paid much attention to their surroundings, and found they were in front of The Venetian. The clock tower watched over them, golden lights making it glow in contrast to the night sky.

"How about we go sit over there?" Natalia asked, nodding toward the rows of steps overlooking the world-famous Grand Canal, where visitors could ride an authentic Italian gondola through the resort. The steps were right behind the area they docked the gondolas when not in use.

Since it was almost midnight, the gondoliers had already closed up shop.

They crossed the bridge that connected the Strip to the Venetian and made their way to the bottom of the steps, sitting right along the fence separating them from the water, blue light glowing underneath the surface.

Adrian let out a long sigh as he lowered himself to sit down next to Natalia. "They never warn you how bad your legs are going to hurt walking around Vegas."

"That's why they give you so much booze, so your legs can go numb and you just keep going."

They laughed before falling silent for the first time since they started walking back at the MGM Grand.

The breeze was light, but strong enough to run subtle ripples through the water. Classic Italian jazz played softly through nearby speakers. Droves of people strode along the Strip, yet they were the only two on the steps.

"I'm sorry for ignoring you all this time," Adrian said. "I really enjoy talking with you. It's easy."

Oh my God, Natalia thought. *Is he hitting on me?*

"I like talking to you, too. Imagine all the conversations we missed out on while you were being an asshole."

She said this with a smile.

Adrian returned a tight-lipped grin, but kept his gaze ahead to the water. "I may not be tall, but I am dark and handsome."

Definitely hitting on me. You hate him. You hate him. You hate him. Don't let the rum change that.

Natalia's heart raced, suddenly pounding the distant drums of passion.

Adrian looked up and locked eyes with Natalia. His presence consumed her. They sat on the Venetian steps, alone in their own world. Months of tension had instantly heated up, ready to burst into flames.

Natalia swallowed hard. Adrian gulped. His face inched closer to hers.

No one will ever know, right? It can be our little secret.

She leaned in closer, their faces six inches apart.

Time stopped and neither of them moved any closer for what seemed an eternity. They were both feeling out the situation that had just taken a drastic turn.

Nothing had happened yet.

They could stop right here and let this forever linger as an awkward moment.

But neither pulled back. Both blew right past the mental roadblocks, trying to divert the inevitable.

They met in the middle and their lips touched, first skimming against each other in one last plea to turn back, to no avail.

Adrian pressed his lips harder into Natalia's, and she pushed back. The kiss shot sparks through her chest. All hatred temporarily ceased.

What am I doing*?!*

They pulled apart. Adrian with a dumbfounded smile stuck on his face.

Natalia grinned back.

No words needed to be spoken. She could still taste him on her lips. And she liked it.

"Shall we walk back?" Adrian asked, his voice wavering.

Natalia nodded, a nervous lump forming in her throat that prevented her from speaking.

She had just been blindsided, but one thing became clear.

Everything had just changed forever.

CHAPTER *Eight*

Oh my God, what have I done? Adrian asked himself once his lips parted from Natalia's. *Did I really just kiss her? How did this even happen? I still have a girlfriend! I'm a cheating scumbag. I told myself I would never do such a thing, but here I am.*

They held hands while walking back down the Strip to the hotel. Even with his conscience having a complete meltdown, he couldn't help it. Something about talking to Natalia, feeling her lips on his, and now her fingers intertwined with his own, all felt so natural.

But it can't be. We really just met, if you think about it. It's just the rum. And kissing? And still holding hands?

If his girlfriend happened to walk up to them right now, how would this all look?

Adrian shook his head free of the thought. That wasn't going to happen. But did that excuse his actions? It was wrong to kiss Natalia. He knew that much. But where exactly was the line drawn? Some might consider the very fact he was on this trip with another woman as cheating.

Who was in charge of rules and ethics? Adrian wanted a word with them.

Girlfriend of five years, *you fool. It's not like you just got into a new relationship and had a change of heart. You've built something over those five years. You graduated high school together. Suffered through a long-distance relationship when her father forced her to choose a school at least three hours away. All to come out on the other side, still together. Did you already forget how proud you both were to have made it through that? The biggest challenge of your relationship. And to throw it all away for what, kissing a stranger in Las Vegas?*

Adrian had never felt so disgusted with himself. He needed a shower to cleanse his mind, body, and soul.

They walked, still holding hands, in silence. Was Natalia having a moment of her own? Trying to understand what the hell had just happened?

You need to go back to your room, call Barbara, and tell her what happened.

He couldn't do that. It was one o'clock in the morning, two o'clock in Denver. Calling her now would only cause a panic.

He'd call her in the morning, just as he had done every day so far on this trip. That didn't need to change. *But I can't just tell her this happened. Not over the phone, and not while I'm still here with Natalia for three more days. That's just asking for trouble. All I need to do is pretend this didn't happen. Maybe if I drink enough tonight, I can forget the entire evening and have it erased from my mind.*

But Adrian knew it was too late for that. It had already happened. Blacking out would only erase whatever happened from this point forward. Besides, you could erase thoughts, but not feelings. When their lips touched, he *felt* something he hadn't in years. But what?

It was too pure to label it a quick flash of lust. Too meaningful to chalk it up as a "heat of the moment" type of crime.

It's just something different. Someone different. It could have been anyone. Tonight just happened to be Natalia. Who I hate, right? So there's nothing to really fuss over. It was an accident. It won't happen again.

Even telling himself it was all a mistake, Adrian couldn't physically remove his hand from Natalia's.

"So," Adrian said, *needing* to break the silence.

"So," Natalia replied, laughing.

A hollow pit formed in Adrian's chest. His mind and heart seemed to race each other as part of a battle of confusion. He hadn't been paying attention to where they were walking, his thoughts on another planet entirely. They had left the Venetian in the dust, already approaching the Flamingo.

"I think we need to talk about what just happened," Adrian said.

"Do we?" Natalia asked, tightening her grip on his hand.

"Are you drunk?"

"No. Are you?"

"No. I guess that eliminates one possibility—this was not a drunken mistake."

"You think it was a mistake?" She raised an eyebrow.

Even with the accusing tone of her question, Natalia held firmly to his hand, as if daring him to let go. He couldn't.

"No, that's not what I'm saying. Quite the opposite. I just—I have a girlfriend. Yes, I know, I just told you how bad things are going with her, and I plan to call it off. But I still feel wrong. I'd be a mess if I knew she was out tonight kissing some other guy."

"That's fair. Should we stop spending time together on this trip?"

The question caught him off guard. That would certainly help his conscience, but he didn't want to spend time away from Natalia. In fact, he wanted to spend every second he could with her. It had only been one night of getting to know each other, and he *needed* to know more. She had been one of the great mysteries in his life until this trip, and now he had a prime opportunity to shed some light on Natalia. He'd be foolish to squander it.

"Uh, no," Adrian finally replied. "I don't think that's necessary. Let's just slow things down. I want to keep hanging out. Do you?"

The question felt like a leap of faith once the words left his lips. A gamble he hadn't taken when talking to a woman for many years now. And he loved the rush, the same swirl of emotions each time he watched the little white ball *whir!* around the roulette wheel.

"Well, yes I do," she replied, confident in her answer.

Relief shot through Adrian's body, even though he had braced for an opposite response.

"Is that okay with *you*?" Natalia asked back with a giggle. "You're the one having a panic attack right now."

Adrian let out a laugh beyond his control. "Of course it's okay with me. I'm just trying to make sense of everything that happened just now."

"Right."

They kept walking down the Strip, moving at a hurried pace despite being the end of a long day. Their hands never separated, minus quick moments going up and down the escalators connecting the bridges that spanned from hotel to hotel.

They reached Planet Hollywood and turned away from the Strip, down a side street where their hotel waited a block away.

"What do we have planned tomorrow?" Natalia asked.

"I think me and Denver are playing in a morning tournament. The rest of the day is free."

"I see. I'll find somewhere to have breakfast with Caroline, then we can plan to meet up later. Maybe around lunch time?"

"Plan for a later lunch, in case one of us is making a deep run, and you have a deal."

Adrian's heart raced at the thought of already getting to see Natalia again tomorrow. Part of him wanted to skip the tournament and spend the morning with her, too. The other part of him reminded about his girlfriend back home, and he should certainly play in the tournament and avoid Natalia like the plague.

"Sounds good," Natalia said as they walked to the entrance of their hotel lobby. "I had a great time tonight."

"So did I."

Before they stepped in, they paused with their faces inches apart, the temptation of a goodnight kiss begging to be had.

But neither of them made the move, and let the tension remain.

"I'll see you tomorrow," Natalia said. "Good luck in the tournament."

"Have a good night."

Natalia stepped into the hotel while Adrian remained outside.

He pulled out his cell phone and dialed Barbara, knowing he should have waited until the morning. But if he didn't clear his conscience right now, he'd never fall asleep.

"Hello?" she answered, voice groggy from a deep sleep.

"Hey!" Adrian said, trying to sound positive and energetic. Definitely not guilty, like the thoughts pounding on the door of his conscience. "I know you're sleeping. But I missed you. I was just getting ready to go to bed and wanted to say good night."

"Really?" Her voice remained devoid of any energy. "Is everything okay?"

"Everything is great!" Adrian said with a forced glee.

"Are you having fun with *Natalia*?" Barbara asked. The amount of disgust she said Natalia's name with sent a shiver down Adrian's back.

Does she actually suspect something is going on?

Barbara had made it clear she wasn't too pleased with Adrian going to Vegas with another woman, but he had assured her they would spend little time together. Adrian was going to gamble and make money. Natalia was simply an accessory to the trip. *How wrong was I?*

"Natalia?" Adrian asked, keeping his tone calm. "I've hardly seen her. I just got back in from a late night playing blackjack and was thinking of you."

I'm going to hell. Who am I?

"That's sweet," Barbara said dismissively, "but I have an exam in the morning. I need to get back to sleep."

"Of course. I'm so sorry." *She knows.*

"Don't worry about it. We'll talk tomorrow. I love you."

"I love you, too."

They hung up, and the reality smacked Adrian so abruptly across the face he might have fallen over had he not taken a seat on the wooden bench next to the hotel entrance. He felt absolutely *nothing* when talking to his girlfriend of five years. No guilt. No shame. Not even love.

Have I already moved on?

CHAPTER *Nine*

THE REST of the week in Vegas followed a similar pattern. They spent the days with Denver and Caroline, gambling, eating, and enjoying the company. Adrian and Natalia kept the heat under wraps in front of their older friends. After dinner each night, they were then free to roam the Strip, just the two of them.

The kiss outside the Venetian on Monday was no drunken fluke—not that either of them had really believed that. Once they were alone in the evenings, they became inseparable. Holding hands. Kissing at every moment that presented itself, and those that did not.

Natalia was due to fly back home to Colorado on Friday, which meant that they spent an emotional evening on Thursday, with more questions than answers as their return to real life loomed.

Adrian still had a girlfriend. Natalia had just gotten out of a relationship and was entirely focused on starting her new career. Neither were in a position to return home and change their lives, no matter how tempting it might have seemed after a perfect week together.

Somehow they had to act like everything was normal, even while agreeing to portray a regular friendship at the office.

Monday morning, Adrian walked in at one minute until eight o'clock, settled into his desk, and then strolled over to the water cooler.

"Good morning, Natalia," he said.

"Good morning. How was your flight home?"

Adrian filled his bottle, and for the first time, he remained at the cooler to keep chatting.

"It was good," he said, leaning against the five-gallon jug. "No issues. Spent all of yesterday lying around. Didn't even unpack. I don't know if I can ever do seven days in Vegas again. That was… a lot."

Natalia giggled. "Five days was more than enough for me. I can't imagine two more."

Adrian lowered his voice and leaned in closer. "I mean, I wouldn't have minded if the trip ran a little longer, assuming everyone from our group got to stay."

Natalia grinned. "I know you have a thing for Caroline, but my goodness, try to keep it a secret."

They broke into laughter that echoed around the quiet call center.

Melissa wandered over from the back row. "Look at you two," she said with a cheesy smile. "What happened in Vegas?!"

"Nothing," Adrian snapped, a tinge of guilt in his voice.

Natalia played it off much more smoothly. "We discussed our issues. Everything is fine between us. You might even call us friends."

"Well, I'll be damned," Melissa said, throwing an arm around Adrian's shoulder. "You two are the only ones who didn't get along. This is exciting for all of us! We've kind of felt like kids in a divorce. Couldn't ever invite you both to the same gatherings. Now we can?"

"What? Really?" Adrian asked. "What events have I not been invited to?"

"Nothing important," Melissa said. "All that matters is we can all hang out now. So exciting!"

Melissa clapped her hands and squealed like a giddy child before slapping Adrian on the back and returning to her desk.

"Well, there you go," Adrian said. "I guess everyone knows we're friends now."

"It's not such a bad thing, is it?" Natalia asked.

"Of course not." Adrian's desk phone rang, prompting an eye roll before he begrudgingly left to answer it.

Okay. That wasn't so bad. Things will be different. That's fine.

Natalia expected some tension upon their return to work. Sexual tension, perhaps. Or even resuming her hatred toward him, at least on some level. People were bound to change their attitudes based on their surroundings, and she wouldn't have been surprised if Adrian changed his mind at the last minute and opted to leave what happened in Vegas, in Vegas and go back to shunning her while in the office.

But clearly, he had embraced their new friendship. Or was he only holding on to the kiss they shared? Or the hundreds that followed in such a brief span after?

Natalia would never admit it, but she'd had a dream last night about Adrian. They were kissing on the Venetian steps, and as could only happen in a dream, there wasn't a single other person in Las Vegas for this special moment.

Just thinking about it now flushed her body with heat, and she couldn't deny the desire throbbing in her chest when she thought back to that first night in Vegas.

"I need to see Adrian, Melissa, and Natalia in my office, please," Lopez called out from his doorway, his voice much too perky for the start of the workday.

Everyone else in the call center looked around at the three who had been called upon. Denver let out a half-hearted chuckle. "Good luck in there," he muttered. "Dead man walkin'."

"Oh, Denver, stop," Lopez said, returning a laugh. "After all these years and you still crack those jokes."

The three filed into the office, and Lopez left the doors open, an instant sign that the conversation wouldn't be too serious. Three chairs were against the glass wall, and Melissa took one on the end, probably on purpose to force Adrian and Natalia to sit next to each other in the two open seats.

Lopez's office was stuffed with filing cabinets against the wall behind him. A messy pile of papers was scattered across his desk, burying the framed family pictures lining the edge.

Natalia had fought off the thoughts that had visited her in the middle of the night. She even kept them at bay while Adrian had chatted with her just a few minutes ago.

But just now, as they sat down, one of Adrian's fingers gently brushed against her hand on the armrest as he positioned himself in the seat.

She had read somewhere that when someone of the opposite sex makes physical contact with you, no matter how subtle, you will always feel it. She had just felt the accidental stroke from Adrian's hand, and was certain he had felt it, too.

Last night wasn't just thoughts. It was a dream that left nothing to the imagination. In the dream, she had a room in the Venetian, where they had returned for a long night of intimacy. She already knew how his lips felt pressed against hers and applied that same sensation to the rest of her body.

She had woken at four o'clock in a drenching sweat, despite the house being freezing—her mother preferred the climate of an igloo. The dream had felt too real, and the part that bothered her the most was that she enjoyed it. When she fell back asleep—after an hour—she *wanted* to return to that dream. Even though she had plenty of doubt that any of it could become a reality.

It's not like we're in a relationship, she told herself as she drove to work this morning. *He still has his little girlfriend, and I don't even know where my life is going to take me. Why does this have to be so complicated? It was much easier to hate him before this got all messy.*

"Natalia?" Lopez called, snapping her out of her impromptu day dream. "Are you with us?"

Adrian and Melissa were both looking at her, eyebrows raised in concern.

"I'm sorry," Natalia replied, blinking her eyes awake. "I missed what you said."

Lopez grinned. "I said we have a project that I'd like the three of you to work on. Will you be able to get started on it today?"

Natalia shook her head free of Adrian. Free of the fantasies. And the hate.

"Yes, count me in."

"Perfect," Lopez said, pointing to a stack of boxes piled up beside his desk. "It's not just you three, keep in mind. We have multiple mailers we need to get sent out on behalf of groups and season tickets. You three will be working one, and I'll group everyone else to work on the others. We need to have these in the mail tomorrow. A little over one thousand mailers. I expect you'll finish sometime tomorrow morning. Any questions?"

Natalia smiled and shook her head, sure to make it obvious that she was paying attention. Everyone liked to complain when these types of projects came down the pipeline, but Natalia didn't mind them one bit. It was busy work, sure, but it was mindless and she could fly through the task much faster than anyone else in the call center.

"What's the deal?" Melissa asked. "What are we doing exactly?"

"One box has a letter. Another has the colorful mailer. And the third has the envelopes. You'll need to put the letter and mailer together, fold them into thirds to stuff into the envelope, seal it, then put the mailing labels on."

"Seal with our tongues?" Melissa asked, plenty of sass in her voice.

"I'm afraid so. I looked for some glue sticks but we don't have any. And they don't like when we use tape."

"Lovely," Melissa said, not hiding the dread in her voice. "Adrian, you want to take the sealing part, or should we take turns?"

Everyone knew Natalia was the fastest at folding and stuffing the envelopes, and wouldn't dare waste her talent to lick envelopes, no matter how awful the adhesive tasted.

"I can handle a split," Adrian said. "Unless you'd like a turn, Natalia?"

"I'll stuff everything," she said. "I can be done before we leave today."

Natalia had no interest in doing this pointless work beyond one day. Her portion would be done, and she'd return home with a clear conscience.

Hopefully *without* thoughts of Adrian.

CHAPTER *Ten*

Towards the end of the following workday, the same three were called into their manager's office. This time, Lopez closed the door while they took the same seats as yesterday.

"We have a problem," Lopez said, not bothering with pleasantries. "The wrong address labels were put on the envelopes. Adrian, I know you were doing the labels. Did you grab the wrong ones? There were two piles of addresses. One for season tickets, another for groups. All the ones you did yesterday had the group labels on the envelopes, but season ticket information inside."

Natalia's stomach sank. Adrian had been doing all the labels after Melissa sealed them. The sheets of address labels each had a small mark in the upper right corner with an S or G to signify which label belonged to which group of customers. Natalia had informed Melissa that they were stuffing the season ticket information, but that message had never been relayed to Adrian, whose face now resembled a white sheet of paper.

Granted, he should have asked, but it was far too late for that.

The mood in Lopez's office had shifted to one of blame, all thanks to the accusatory tone coming from their manager.

"I—" Adrian started.

"It was my fault," Natalia said. "I grabbed the labels for Adrian while he was moving all the boxes to my desk. I handed him the wrong ones."

Adrian snapped his head around to look at Natalia, but she kept her gaze forward on Lopez, who frowned. He almost seemed disappointed that the blame was misdirected.

"Is that so?" Lopez asked, leaning back in his seat and crossing his arms. "Well, Natalia, this is a costly mistake, both in shipping expenses and in the time our teams are going to spend calling all these accounts to let them know about the mix-up." Lopez sounded deflated.

"Are we going to need to do them all again?" Melissa asked, using her charming Southern tone in an attempt to lighten the mood.

"We haven't decided yet. We'll figure that out before the weekend, so stay tuned. I wanted to bring this to your attention and learn the whole story. Seems like it was an honest mistake."

Angst crept into their manager's voice. With only Natalia to blame, he had nowhere to go. He knew it didn't matter that Natalia made the mistake, since she was already on the job hunt.

"I'm so sorry," Natalia said, feigning her best apologetic voice. "I can't believe I messed this up."

"Let's pay attention to the little details going forward, okay? You three can head out now."

The clock had struck five o'clock while they were in the office, the rest of their coworkers having already cleared out by the time they returned to their desks to pack up their things.

Natalia felt Adrian's eyes burning into the back of her head while she loaded her purse, but she didn't turn around, instead slipping out the door next to the water cooler.

Adrian met her in the elevator lobby, not speaking until the glass doors closed behind them.

"Why did you do that?" he asked in a whisper as they stood shoulder to shoulder. She could still hear the shock and worry in his voice.

Natalia smiled, staring ahead as the elevator doors parted and they stepped in.

"You have a future here," she said. "I don't. If all goes well, I'll be out of here before the summer. It's the least I can do."

"No one's ever done something like that for me." Adrian spoke in a way she had never heard before, a mixture of awe and pure gratitude.

"Well, I guess there's a first time for everything." She nudged her elbow into his arm.

"How can I repay you? I owe you big time."

"You don't need to do anything. It was a favor. That's what friends do, right?"

Adrian nodded, looking at the floor as he searched for his next words. "Let me give you a ride to the light rail station. It's not out of my way at all."

Natalia knew it was, indeed, out of his way. Adrian lived in Thornton and she lived in Aurora. The light rail stop closest to the stadium was ten blocks southeast, well out of the way from how Adrian would normally get on the freeway to drive home.

"Okay," she said. "That would be great."

They walked through the stadium's underground tunnel without a word, tension filling the silence between them.

Once they stepped outside, it was like someone had ripped the tape off Adrian's mouth.

"Seriously," he said. "Thank you so much. I still can't believe you just did that. For me."

"It's no big deal. Really."

"No, that's where you're wrong. It *is* a big deal. Ever since I came back into the call center after working with the groups team, it's felt like they're trying to find anything to pin on me. I'm not sure why, but Matt seems to have it out for me."

Matt was the manager of the group ticketing department where Adrian had worked during the prior season.

"Well, I'm glad I could help." They continued into the parking lot, Natalia pulling her purse off her shoulder as they approached the cars.

"If I can just hang on here for a few more months, I might land a job with a different team. I applied to work for the Padres in their call center as a team lead, since I apparently will never get that type of role here."

They reached Adrian's car and settled inside with Adrian starting it up and beginning the long journey around the back side of the stadium.

"You're moving to San Diego?" Natalia asked, suddenly struck by how much she didn't like the thought of Adrian leaving.

"If they offer me the job, yeah. Great city, and I've heard they're one of the best teams to work for in the entire league."

"I see."

Easier to just hate him. That way, when he leaves, you'll be overcome with joy.

But it wasn't that simple. Plenty of hate was leftover. She wasn't going to completely forgive him after months of shunning and mind games just because they had one fun week together. The hate had softened, sure, and she could even admit to liking certain aspects of him. If he moved out of state, maybe that would be better for them both.

"What is your goal in life?" Natalia asked, trying to distract her mind as they exited the stadium grounds and joined the bustling downtown traffic. "What's your dream?"

"Well, like you said, I want a future in baseball. It just doesn't seem like that future will be at the Rockies. I want to work my way up to becoming a general manager. Running a baseball team at the highest level has to be the best job in the world."

"And how do you get there?"

"I need to get out of ticketing and into baseball operations. That can be anything. Player development, scouting. There are lots of entry-level jobs I can get into. And once you're in there, you just have to bust your ass and climb the ladder. It will probably take a couple of decades to get anywhere close. Keep in mind, there are only thirty GM jobs up for grabs, and thousands of people vying for them. I understand it's a long shot, but it's one I want to pursue."

"That's good. Maybe a change of scenery at the Padres will help." They pulled up to a red light and Adrian turned his head to lock eyes with her.

"Definitely. No baggage there. I can have a fresh start and get back on track to pursuing my dreams. I just have to graduate college in May, and I'll be set. There is simply no one working in baseball operations without a college degree, unless they were a former player."

"Well, I hope what I did today can help you reach that goal."

Adrian laughed. "It definitely didn't hurt. I just need to survive until graduation. I'm still going to apply for a role in baseball ops at the Rockies, but I highly doubt I'll even get an interview."

"I'm sure you'll be fine, no matter what happens."

Adrian smiled. She had charmed him with that comment. "So, what's the deal with your job search?"

Natalia shrugged. "Lots of applications and phone interviews. Virtually no follow up beyond that."

"Why do you think that's so?"

"Hard to say. It's a very competitive job market. I'm a woman fighting for a job in an industry dominated by men. I'm newly graduated. Combine all of that, and it makes my search a little harder."

"Any company would be so lucky to have you. I mean, you are the queen of stuffing envelopes."

Natalia cackled, shaking her head. "You're stupid."

Adrian laughed back, their conversation natural and free-flowing. They arrived at the light rail station, lines of people already forming for their return trip home.

"Thanks again," Adrian said, reaching out and placing a hand on Natalia's forearm. There was no mistaking that intentional physical contact, his touch somehow transporting her back to Vegas. And her dream.

It felt like the temperature in the car had just risen ten degrees. Natalia needed to get out.

"Don't worry about it," she said, opening the door. "I'll see you tomorrow?"

"Of course. Have a good night."

CHAPTER *Eleven*

ADRIAN HAD a long talk with himself during the drive home that evening. The day had proven to be one of his worst during his time with the Rockies, yet Natalia had made it all better. Ever since they had returned from the trip and resumed their regular lives, Adrian constantly thought about her.

Even after visits to Barbara's apartment, he'd return home and lie down, thinking about Natalia. The walls were closing around his existing relationship, and it was time to man up and call things off before those same walls crushed his very existence.

He hadn't planned on doing it when he woke up this morning, but the thought smothered his mind all day, building to the point of actually making the decision during the drive home. He and Barbara already had dinner plans at his apartment tonight. Adrian just needed to muster the courage to have this most unfortunate conversation.

No cliches. No mention of anything in Vegas. Certainly no mention of Natalia.

This needed to be about Adrian. He wasn't leaving Barbara for Natalia. But the latter had opened his eyes to the possibilities of a new world. A new life. Having outgrown his high school sweetheart was a bitter pill to swallow, but that was the best he could understand of what was taking place in his heart.

"And she's already here," Adrian said under his breath, turning into his complex and seeing Barbara's blue Buick in the parking spot right outside his front door. "I don't even get to prepare the place. Okay, here we go. Best thing that can happen is she admits to having similar feelings. It'll still hurt, but it won't be as bad. Worst case scenario, the opposite is true and things get messy."

Adrian pulled into the open spot next to her, and she looked over with a wide smile and a wave. His roommate, Jerome, wouldn't return from work until around ten o'clock. No interruptions.

Adrian stepped out of his car, Barbara doing the same.

"Hey, mister," she said, brushing back her blonde hair.

Dammit, Adrian thought. Barbara's tone was chipper. *This isn't going to be easy.*

"Hay is for horses," he said, earning the obligatory chuckle from the girl who had laughed at all his stupid jokes for the past five years.

She shuffled to the door and waited, giving him a quick kiss before he jiggled his keys to unlock it.

"How was your day?" she asked once they stepped inside.

"Another day in the dream," he said, his altercation with Lopez—and rescue by Natalia—completely erased from his mind for the moment. He could barely think straight, planning how he wanted to end this long-term relationship, let alone remember what he had for lunch.

Whenever Adrian had to deliver bad news, he had long preferred to "rip the band-aid off" and not beat around the bush. He supposed this approach would work best tonight, too. Any other way and Barbara was sure to sniff out the truth, which would then put him on the defensive.

"How was your day?" Adrian asked, looking his girlfriend up and down. Could he really leave her? Faced with the harsh reality in front of him, it no longer seemed so simple. She was his first love. They had been through so much together. Their relationship had been more than high school puppy love. It was as real as it could be for teenagers coming into adulthood. She had helped him through his parents' divorce, easily the darkest of days in his life. His own sister had confided in Barbara about the confusion surrounding her sexuality, well before she had told anyone else in the family. This breakup was going to have wide, painful ripples, and part of him thought it would all be worth it to suck it up and continue the relationship. He wasn't happy, but he wasn't miserable. They were just stuck in the limbo of going through the motions. Didn't every romance eventually reach that point? Were the couples who remained married for fifty years simply the ones who pushed through the boring stretch? Did they ever find that excitement again? That spark? Or was it all just putting your head down and powering through?

Or maybe some people are only meant to be in your life for a particular reason. To help us grow. To help us through the bad times. Just because it hurts in the end, doesn't mean it's not worth it.

"Are you listening?" Barbara asked, waving her hands in front of Adrian's blank eyes.

"I'm sorry, what?" Adrian shook his head, startled.

"You asked how my day was, and I was trying to tell you. Are you okay?"

"Sorry. It was a long day. I'm listening now. Tell me all about it." They stood at the kitchen counter while Adrian fished out food from the refrigerator.

Barbara scrunched her face in confusion, bright blue eyes searching for a tell. She had known him long enough to know when something was bothering him, no matter what he said.

"Okay," she continued, sounding unsure of herself. "I had a full morning of classes, then went downtown to work a few hours over the lunch rush. Made decent enough tips. I'm becoming so overwhelmed with some of my assignments, though. I have to write a ten-page essay for one class, a five-page one for another, all on top of regular homework and reading."

Don't worry, you'll have plenty of free time soon enough.

Adrian felt sick that he even had such a mean thought. He suspected the evening would go as smooth as sandpaper. Barbara was in a plenty normal mood. Normal routine.

"Should we eat?" she asked, eyes still boring into him, looking for a clue.

"Yes." Adrian served two bowls of leftover spaghetti, ran them through the microwave, and topped them off with grated parmesan before settling at the table with Barbara.

He couldn't have had any less of an appetite. Barbara chowed down her spaghetti. Not a care in the world. They had planned for dinner and watching a couple of movies. She had brought her bag to stay overnight in case it got too late, as was often the case.

Forcing bites of spaghetti down his throat was torturing Adrian, but he wasn't ready to pull the trigger and lay out the bad news. It was only fair both of them had a full stomach, because there was no saying how the next few days of mourning might affect both of their appetites.

Barbara finished her bowl of pasta in about fifteen minutes. Meanwhile, Adrian poked around his for thirty minutes before declaring he was too full to finish.

"Full?" Barbara asked, suspicion now entirely in her voice. "Since when? Are you sure you're okay?"

Adrian gulped. Those walls were closing. He always could mask his emotions, but not hide them from himself—or Barbara, apparently.

"Yes, I'm fine," he said, heart pounding all the way to his eardrums. "Just a late lunch today. And we are eating kind of early."

It was barely 6:15, and they had just finished dinner. Would this evening ever end?

"You wanna go watch a movie now?" she asked, standing up from the table and carrying the dishes to the sink.

I can say yes and put off the inevitable for another couple of hours. But I still have to do it. Do I really want to sit through a whole movie with this anxiety ready to burst out of my chest? Get it over with. Both of our lives are going to drastically change tonight. No point in delaying that fact.

Adrian's legs bounced so wildly that even he noticed, yet he still couldn't do anything to contain them. He thought he might vomit for a moment, nervous hiccups rising through his throat like agitated bubbles.

"Or not?" Barbara said, returning to the table. "Seriously, what's going on?"

Don't say 'We need to talk.' Cliche.

"Can you sit down? I need to talk to you about something."

Despite not using the classic breakup line, a ghastly look swept over Barbara's face, turning her more pale than usual. "Um, what's happening? This isn't what I think it is, right?"

Adrian swallowed hard. *She already knows. Rip. The. Band-aid. Off.* "Just… sit down. Please."

Barbara drew a deep breath and did just that, bracing herself like a death row convict readying to face the electric chair. Her eyes glossed over with a thin film of moisture.

How could she possibly know? Have I been that distant lately?

None of that was for Adrian to decide. He had no control over how his actions were perceived by others. If Barbara had thought something was off before tonight, she would have already mentioned it.

He laid out a hand on the table. Barbara stared at it for a moment, clearly torn about whether she should grab it. She did.

Her usual soft touch graced his fingertips, but it still lacked that perfect feeling he had experienced several days earlier.

"Barbara," he started. "I don't know how to say any of this, but I've been going through some changes."

She shook her head, that moisture in her eyes welling to a tear streaming down her cheek.

"Are you serious right now?" she whispered. "This is really how it ends?"

Her last sentence wasn't directed to Adrian, but to herself. She pulled her hand away from his.

"Look," Adrian said, staring at his empty hand and wondering how long it would remain that way. "I want you to know it's not personal. There's nothing you did. Nothing wrong with you. This is all about me and my problems. I'm lost right now. I don't even know what I want out of life any more. My dream job seems like an impossibility. I'm graduating in a few months with no clue what I'm supposed to do with a business degree."

Barbara gasped. "And you don't think I'm going through the same stuff? Where have you been? I'm graduating, too. And I don't have a foot in the door in my dream industry already. I'm a *waitress*. Remember? I have to start from the ground up wherever I end up going. You've already been doing that these last four years. So don't sit there and throw a pity party."

She wiped the tears from her eyes, already bloodshot and swelling with rage and sorrow.

"I'm not asking for pity," Adrian said, remaining calm despite Barbara's rising anger. "I'm saying I don't know if I even want a future in baseball anymore."

Barbara scoffed. "Are you *high*?! Are you really about to throw *everything* away from the last five years of your life? For what? Was any of it even worth it?"

Her rage switched to a messy sob in an instant, tears now pouring down her face, pooling at the bottom of her chin before splashing onto the table.

"Barbara, please. I know this isn't easy."

"Easy?! Maybe for you. I've been putting the work into this relationship. You have not. Especially after your Vegas trip. What happened out there? You've been completely different since you got back."

"Nothing happened." The guilt crept back into his thoughts,

pounding on the door of his mind like a bill collector who won't quit. He hadn't confronted the guilt in a couple of days. Did she actually suspect something happened between him and Natalia? She hadn't mentioned her by name. "Actually, yes, something did happen in Vegas. I realized for the first time just how different life is after turning twenty-one. There's an entire world out there we've never experienced before. It opened my eyes."

Barbara's head hung as she stared at the floor. She raised it just enough to lock her wet eyes with Adrian. "And you don't want to experience it with me?"

Her lips quivered as she asked the question. No matter how he tried to beat around the answer, it all boiled down to the same thing she already knew.

"I don't know what I want," Adrian said through the bulging frog forming in his throat.

"You just know that you *don't* want me, right?"

He shook his head. "I told you to not take it personally."

She tossed her hands up. "How could I ever not take this personally? You're my first love. You're dumping me two weeks before our five-year anniversary. We were supposed to graduate and travel together this summer. We've been talking about that for a year. I just—it feels like it was all for nothing. We're not even splitting up over an argument like normal people. It's one-sided, so you can go find yourself, whatever that means. I don't think I can ever forgive you for this."

She stood up, crossing the room to snatch her backpack that she had put outside of Adrian's bedroom door.

"Where are you going?" Adrian asked.

"What does it matter to you?" She refused eye contact while she scanned the apartment for anything that might have been hers. Her lips quivered, arms trembling.

"Are you even okay to drive right now?"

"I'll take my chances. Clearly I'm not wanted here anymore, so there's no point in sticking around."

Her face was beet red, and the tears hadn't slowed one bit.

Adrian's eyes welled up as Barbara started for the door. Once she left and closed the door, she'd be gone. Potentially forever. He hadn't expected this reality to hit him as hard as it did, but when she swung open the door and stepped outside, that's exactly what happened.

Both were crying.

Barbara turned around and looked him in the eyes one last time, pointing a finger directly at his face. "I don't care what you do, but all I ask is please don't date Natalia."

CHAPTER Twelve

ADRIAN DIDN'T SHOW up to work the next day. Natalia thought he had mentioned that he'd be in, so she checked the schedule and confirmed that he was on it. He hadn't shown any signs of illness the prior day, so it made little sense for him to have called out sick. He had been completely fine when he dropped her off at the light rail station.

She sent him a text at 8:30, asking if he was okay. With no response by noon, she asked Melissa if she had, by chance, heard anything.

"Adrian's in rough shape today," she explained, frowning. "He texted me last night that he broke up with his girlfriend."

Natalia didn't know why, but hearing this news filled her chest with shock. She had known it was coming, but wouldn't he have mentioned it during their drive after work last night?

I thought we were close enough that he'd share these things with me, but apparently not.

"Did he really?" Natalia asked, touching her hand to her lips in surprise.

"Yeah. I don't know the details, just that it happened. It's really too bad."

"He actually mentioned to me in Vegas that things were rocky.

He was contemplating calling things off with her. I'm just surprised he did it so quickly."

"Maybe it's not that quick. Who knows how long he's been considering it? He could've just reached his tipping point." Melissa shrugged and their conversation was cut short by her phone ringing.

Natalia left for her lunch break, going up to the empty third-floor call center for privacy. She pulled out her cell phone and started typing a message to send to Adrian.

Hey, Melissa told me the news. I'm sorry. Let me know if you need anything.

She stared at it, analyzing every word on the screen. Did any part of it seem too aggressive? Too involved? Or worse, too cheerful?

"No exclamation points," she said to herself. "No emojis. It's just a regular message from one friend to another."

Natalia deleted the message.

We're not actually friends. I'm obviously still hungover from whatever that was in Vegas.

She couldn't reach out to him the day after his breakup. If he was struggling enough that he had to call into work, especially considering the thin ice he claimed to already be skating on, then he was definitely in a dark place, mentally.

Adrian would be at his most vulnerable today. Depressed, anxious about the future, although maybe with a sliver of optimism. She could only base this assumption off her own recent breakup. Regardless of which combination of emotions he was experiencing, it was definitely too aggressive for her to reach out. If they hadn't just had their tongues down each other's throats for all of last week, she could take a different approach. But their sudden bonding in Vegas complicated things, no matter how much either refused to accept that simple fact.

"He just got out of a five-year relationship," she whispered to the empty room. "The last thing he needs is to hear from the only other person he's kissed during those five years."

Natalia just realized she had been pacing circles around the office, mind spinning with every possibility. She *wanted* to reach out, just to see how he was doing. It didn't need to be part of some agenda, but how would he receive it in his vulnerable state of mind?

We are *friends. We agreed to be friends, right?*

If that was true, wouldn't he have reached out already? He had informed Melissa, who *was* a true friend of Adrian. Could he have resentment toward Natalia? Maybe the guilt of kissing her and spending all that time together in Vegas is what truly pushed him to the brink.

All this confusion made it feel like they were back to square one, fanning the flames of hate. However, it was difficult to feel anger toward someone suffering. She had her issues with Adrian, sure, but he didn't deserve to go through today with so much pain. His world was shaken, and he didn't know where to go from here. Perhaps hearing from the only person that he had admitted his intentions of breaking up with his girlfriend to, would ease some of that pain.

I can call him. Text messages leave too much up for interpretation. If he hears my voice, he'll know I really am just checking on him.

Natalia burned another five minutes, debating if a phone call was too much, before finally deciding to call him. They had exchanged numbers in Vegas, but this was her first time calling him. Her heart thumped as the callback tone rang in her ear. She had watched him enter her number into his phone and save it under her name. He knew who was calling right now, but would he answer?

"Hello?" Adrian said, his voice smothered in grief.

"Hey," Natalia said, trying to find the balance between positivity and concern. "Melissa told me what happened last night, and I wanted to see how you're doing."

He sniffled. "Oh, been better. Last night might have been the worst night of my life. It wasn't easy. Wasn't fun."

"I'm sorry. I know you were planning on this, but do you still think it was the right move?"

"Hard to say. I guess that depends how the future unravels. Right this moment, I feel absolutely dead inside."

"Is there anything I can do?" Natalia asked, immediately regretting the question.

You're coming on too strong. Just let him vent.

But she felt obligated to help. She was the only person who had even known he was planning this.

But he didn't even tell you. He told Melissa.

They had been friends much longer, so it made sense. And Melissa actually knew Adrian's girlfriend. Natalia was still new to Adrian's life, certainly not at the top of his list to call when going through a rough time.

Would I call him if my breakup happened this week instead of last?

Natalia considered this, knowing she likely wouldn't have reached out to Adrian. For what reason? He had his life; she had hers. They owed nothing to each other, even after burying the hatchet of tension that had plagued them for months.

Yet, the thought of him crying in his bedroom all day actually made her day worse. Once she had peeled back the layers of Mr. Asshole, it had become clear that a kind person waited beneath.

Natalia wanted to smack herself for having such a drastic change of emotions. But it was out of her control. As much as she tried to keep hating Adrian, she simply couldn't.

"I'm coming over after work," she said, slapping her hand to her mouth.

What is wrong with me? It's like I have no control over the words coming out of my lips.

Her heart beat increased to an uncomfortable pace, pounding in her ears so loudly she feared she might not hear Adrian's response to her absurd statement. Heat prickled her face, and beads of nervous sweat formed on her forehead.

She heard Adrian loud and clear when he responded, "I'd love that."

Dear God, what have I gotten myself into?

"Only if it's fine with you," she said, a weak attempt to backpedal from her offer. "And your roommate."

"Fine with me. And Jerome works late. Probably won't even get home until around midnight."

"Okay, great. I'll see you later."

Natalia couldn't hang up the phone fast enough, not giving Adrian a chance to respond.

"Seriously," she said to herself, throwing her hands up and gawking at the ceiling. "What have I done?"

She understood the risk she was taking by visiting Adrian while his past relationship had ended hours ago.

The ex might even show up while she was there, desperate for a last attempt to save their bond, like the ending of a romantic comedy. Only no one would laugh if Natalia was there. It could even turn ugly in a hurry. She would be there only as a friend, but an enraged ex-girlfriend would certainly not see it that way.

Call him back and cancel. It's too soon.

She pondered this, but figured that might only add to Adrian's sorrow at this point. She had heard the slightest tinge of excitement in his voice when she suggested stopping by after work.

Natalia shook her head, disgusted with herself. She had never acted like this. Why was she taking a gamble by inserting herself into Adrian's life during such a critical moment?

She drew in a deep breath before returning to work for the rest of the afternoon, nervous for her visit that loomed in just a few hours.

CHAPTER *Thirteen*

SHE PARKED in the open space in front of Adrian's apartment and killed the headlights immediately. A hot pizza sat in the passenger seat. She figured Adrian's favorite food could lift his spirit. She also brought a two-liter of Coke, his favorite soda, and realized how much she had learned about him during their quick week together in Vegas.

He loved horror movies and video games, and she'd suggest they do both. At the very least, he'd have a couple hours of not feeling down on himself. Just maybe, she could provide a bit of normalcy for what had been an awful day.

Why do I do this? Always taking care of others. Always worried about making everyone else happy. What about me?

Natalia had long been this way. As the oldest of three siblings, she was the natural caretaker for her younger brother and sister. Even outside of the family, people had always come to her for advice. Since middle school all the way through college, dealing with friendships, romance, roommates, and even her extended network in the university's color guard and engineering program, everyone always came to her.

She shouldered the burden, figuring the world simply needed people like her. She was the strong one, and that attracted other people's problems, because as far as they were concerned, she didn't have problems of her own.

Natalia needed her own Natalia in her life, and that was something she hadn't found. She was only strong because she had to put on that façade, often worried what people would think if she didn't appear to have her life together.

She had never been entirely sure she wanted a career in engineering. Her parents had simply suggested the profession because it made good money, but did that even matter if her life wasn't fulfilled by what she would do on a daily basis? She could have gone anywhere in the world for college, but stayed close to home. Doing so resulted in less college debt, which, looking back on now, hardly made a difference. The receipts were just as astronomical as if she had gone out of state.

If she could go back and start all over, she probably would have done something entirely different. Perhaps something in the arts or literature. Something that didn't guarantee a high-paying job, but who cared? What did it matter what was in her bank account?

The biggest hole in her life right now was not having someone to speak about these things with. She had a few close friends who were in her same situation, but that resulted in more of a shared venting.

Adrian had opened up to her about his goals and dreams, and even though she didn't reciprocate, she felt she could have. He was focused on his future, and had a plan for how to get there. It even included working in an industry that paid near poverty level for most positions until you reached the top. No money, but a *purpose*. A calling. For someone who had difficulties approaching and speaking to new people, Adrian was intensely comfortable with himself as a person. He understood who he was to the core, and where he was going, something Natalia wasn't sure she had ever felt.

Stop it, I'm just building him up more. I'm here to help him through a tough time, not praise him.

She had spoken enough to herself, grabbing the pizza and stepping out of the car with determination. When she knocked on the door, she only had to wait a few seconds before Adrian swung it open, dressed in baggy sweatpants and a hoodie, with dark, heavy circles under his bloodshot eyes.

"Hey," he said, looking at her, then down to the pizza. "What's that?"

"Dinner," she said, offering a grin. "I hope you don't mind, but I thought maybe you hadn't eaten much today."

Adrian smiled, an expression that radiated gratitude. "I actually haven't eaten since Pop-Tarts for breakfast. Is it already dinner time?" He slapped a hand against his forehead. "My God, this is so embarrassing. I've literally lost track of time."

"Can I come in?"

"Of course. I'm sorry." He moved aside in a hurry, clearing the way for Natalia.

She stepped into his apartment for the first time, entering the living room where a leather couch faced a TV in the corner. The dining table and kitchen were both straight ahead, a pile of messy dishes in the sink, a couple of greasy fast food bags on the counter.

Adrian must have caught her looking at the mess, and said, "Don't mind all that. My roommate is kind of a slob."

"It's fine."

"I mean it when I say *kind of*. He actually cleans up like a pro, but only does it like once a week. Let's everything stack up and get messy first. Just how he operates, I guess." He shuffled to the dining table and cleared it of magazines and random junk mail. "Would you like something to drink?"

"Oh shoot! I brought a bottle of Coke and left it in the car." Natalia scurried to the table and placed the pizza box down.

"Oh? I'll go get it," Adrian said, putting up a hand like a stop sign. "I could use the three seconds of fresh air. You get settled in. Grab a couple of glasses—they're in the cupboard to the left of the sink. Just unlock your car for me."

"Take my keys. I need to use the restroom anyway."

Adrian's eyes jumped to the open door on the other side of the dining table and filled with worry. "Just use my bathroom. It's in my bedroom. I'm sure the main one isn't too clean, because you know…my roommate."

"You have your own bathroom in your room? That must be nice."

Adrian chuckled and reached for the keys Natalia had pulled out of her jacket pocket. "I can't complain. Help yourself and I'll be right back with the soda.

He disappeared through the front door before she could even respond, running with a surprising grace and speed.

Two minutes later, they convened in the kitchen, where Natalia rummaged through the cupboards for the glasses, bringing them to the table as Adrian had returned with the Coke.

"Plates?" she asked.

"We have paper plates next to the microwave," he said, a grin on his face as he brought the soda to the table, pulling out a seat for Natalia. "This is so nice of you. Thank you."

"It's nothing," Natalia said, trying to play it off. "Melissa told me what happened this morning, and when I called you on my lunch break, you sounded in pretty rough shape."

"But you just got out of a relationship yourself. Have you even had time to come to terms with that?"

Natalia shrugged. Even Adrian questioned why she prioritized others before herself.

"Like I said, we were on and off for years. Wasn't anywhere near the relationship you had. If anything, this breakup with Brett is just part of the routine."

"If it's routine, then you might get back with him?"

She shrugged again. "I don't have any plans for that. Right now, I'm just happy to be focused on me. Except for tonight, it's all about you. What do you want to do after we eat? Play some 2K? Watch a scary movie?"

Adrian furrowed his brow and smirked. "Who are you, and

what did you do with the girl who was only worried about writing her thesis?"

"Ha! I graduated!" Natalia laughed as they flipped open the pizza box and dug in. "I'm just here to hang out and have a quiet evening."

"And what do you know about NBA 2K?" he asked, crossing his arms and leaning back. "You play?"

Natalia had heard plenty of stories about the guys from the call center having intense 2K tournaments at each other's places. "I'm not any good, but I played basketball through high school. How hard can the video game be?"

Adrian threw his head back and let out an exaggerated laugh. "Let the excuses begin."

Over the next three hours, they finished dinner, played a game of 2K where Adrian blew her out of the water, and talked until nine o'clock.

"I don't know what I'm going to do," Adrian said once the electronics had been turned off. They sat next to each other on the living room couch. "My life has been a certain way for the last five years. It had a routine. And now that's all changed, literally overnight. I'm not too concerned about being single again, even though the thought of dating horrifies me. I guess I'm more bothered by what to do with all my free time. My weekends and evenings are entirely mine again."

"I'm finding myself in that same predicament—just now feel like I'm finally getting the chance to settle into a new routine."

"And what are you doing with your time?" Adrian pulled his feet onto the couch as he curled into a ball, and turned to face Natalia straight on.

"That's the thing. I haven't done anything yet. I work during the day, then go home and start applying for engineering jobs. Job hunting is just awful—it takes up so much time. And it's not really an industry where you can just blast applications. Different firms have different specialties, different qualifications, locations, all sorts of little things. I usually spend a couple hours before dinner researching companies, then a couple hours after dinner to actually submit the applications. By the time I'm done with all that, my brain is fried, so I lay in bed watching TV until I fall asleep. All to wake up the next day and do it again. Wow, I never realized how boring my life is until breaking it down that way."

Adrian laughed. "It's not *boring*. It's just the necessary parts of life that lead you to the fun stuff, right? We all have to do it. Applying for colleges, then jobs, then eventually houses. There's no way around it, so it's best to just accept the struggles, let them be a part of your growth, and move on."

Not much flustered Adrian. Even as he sat here, worried about his future after an emotional roller coaster had rattled his life, he kept a calm mind and *listened* to Natalia, offering her useful advice.

"I can try that," she said. "I don't know if you knew, but I do some modeling for my friend. She has her own fashion line."

The change of subject caught Adrian off guard. "Oh? That's pretty cool. What do you do, exactly? Photo shoots for magazines?"

"Fashion shows, actually. I'm doing one this Saturday night downtown. Would you be interested in coming?"

Adrian raised his eyebrows. "I can't say I've ever been to a fashion show."

Too soon. Dammit, why did I have to invite him the same week of his breakup?! Stupid. Stupid. Stupid.

"I'd love to go," he said. "I can't exactly complain about having a wide open schedule then do nothing about it. And what better time than now to try something new? Count me in."

"Great!" Relief flooded her as soon as she heard the enthusiasm in his response. "I'll get you a ticket. We'll probably go out for drinks afterwards, too."

"Even better."

The mood had veered an entirely different direction from what she had walked into earlier. Adrian asked many questions about her past modeling gigs, showing genuine interest in everything she had to say.

Vegas no longer seemed like a fluke. After a few days of tiptoeing around the lingering awkwardness, they were reconnecting tonight, opening up and sharing more details about their lives.

After another hour passed, Natalia needed to head home. There were still two more days of work left in the week, and she couldn't fall behind on sleep heading into the fashion show on Saturday night.

Adrian led her outside, and they paused in the open doorway.

"I'm really glad you came over tonight," Adrian said. He brushed a hand over her forearm. "I didn't know how much I needed this. No one has ever done anything like this for me, so thank you. You're incredible."

Those words made Natalia's heart race. That heat from Vegas returned so suddenly, she thought it might knock them both over. It had somehow avoided them during their evening together, but now, as they said goodbye, she sensed the mutual urge for a farewell kiss.

Definitely too soon, she reminded herself.

Adrian had been single for twenty-four hours. Now was not the time to complicate matters.

"Good night," she said, giving a warm grin. She could see the same thoughts swimming behind Adrian's green eyes. If he wanted the same thing as her, he was showing even greater restraint. If he leaned in toward her, Natalia didn't know how she'd react.

"Good night," Adrian said, lips pinched tight together. "Drive safe. I'll see you at work tomorrow?"

Natalia nodded and turned around to her car.

Rain started falling. Adrian stood in the doorway until Natalia started up her car and pulled out of the parking lot, only closing the door once she was out of sight.

Her cell phone started ringing in her cupholder, and she

immediately thought it was Adrian. Maybe he was inviting her to come back. Maybe he wanted to throw caution to the wind and have that goodbye kiss. Or maybe he just wanted to keep talking.

She snatched up her phone and saw the name on the flashing screen.

"No," she huffed, shaking the phone in her hand. "Why?"

It was Brett.

She drew a deep breath and answered the phone.

CHAPTER *Fourteen*

She sat in her car, in the parking lot outside of an ice cream shop the following evening.

The workday had passed rather uneventfully—a quiet day with no projects. She and Adrian had lunch with Caroline, Denver, and Melissa, and swapped more stories about Vegas.

When Brett had called the night before, he asked to see her in person tonight. He suggested ice cream if he could have just a few minutes of her time to get some things off his chest.

"Why am I doing this?" Natalia asked aloud.

But she'd agreed to it, and now sat here, once more upset with herself for caving to the pressures of others instead of protecting her own inner peace.

Brett wasn't some random person. They had shared memories together. They had sometimes talked about their future together. And while Natalia was sick of the on-and-off nature of their relationship, she couldn't help but feel hopeful when remembering the good times.

Brett had never mistreated her, but she had always suspected she could have been treated better. Recently, she was understanding exactly what better looked like.

She saw Brett sitting inside the ice cream parlor. Part of her wanted to turn the car around and leave. Never look back. The other part wanted to march in there and see what he had to say. She certainly felt no emotional attachment to Brett—that was why she had called things off. There was nothing he could say that would magically change that.

"All he asked for was thirty minutes to talk," she muttered to herself, opening the car door and stepping out. "Listen, enjoy your ice cream, and get the hell out."

She strolled to the entrance, confidence soaring as she stepped inside, the heavenly smells of waffle cones, ice cream, and sprinkles filling the air. Natalia always thought the North Pole would smell fairly similar to a homey ice cream shop.

"Hey, Natalia!" Brett said, standing and waving from the table against the wall. Two cups of ice cream were already on the table. "I ordered your favorite."

She shuffled to the table and gave Brett a half-hearted hug, seeing the pralines and cream flavor in her cup, a small red spoon sticking out from the scattered rainbow sprinkles. They sat down across from each other.

"So," Natalia said, forcing her most uninterested voice. "What's up?"

Brett smiled. A certain warmth radiated from him, a pure happiness Natalia hadn't seen from him in many years. His usually droopy eyes were now perked up, wide and brown. He didn't look so tired, as she had known him. "First off, thank you for agreeing to sit with me today. I know you didn't have to, but it means a lot. I didn't want to end things how we did. We broke up over the phone, and I think we both deserve better than that."

Natalia scooped ice cream into her mouth while Brett spoke, content to sit back and let him rant.

Brett crossed his fingers together and rested his hands on his chest. "I've been doing a lot of reflecting lately—I guess losing you was all I needed to put things into perspective."

He wants to get back together. Unbelievable.

"I know we haven't had the best relationship, and I see that now. With me in the Marines and you in school, it was hard to stay connected. I took what we had for granted. I was so caught up in my own stuff and figured that you were, too. My mistake was thinking you would still be there through all of it. That wasn't fair of me to expect that of you, and I can see that now."

Brett was actually speaking sense for once. People changed, especially in their twenties, when they were still trying to figure out their path forward.

He reached out a hand across the table, but Natalia only stared at it, taking her next bite of ice cream. He laughed under his breath, shaking his head.

"I'm just trying to talk, Natalia. I'm putting myself out on a limb. When I think of my future, you're always in it. I won't be in the military forever. I have dreams for a future beyond the Marines, and it includes you—I can't imagine anyone else."

Natalia felt the ice cream swirling in her stomach and pushed her cup back. "I'm glad to hear all this," she said, clearing her throat. "Really. It shows a lot of growth. But how can I know it's for real? We've had conversations like this before, but we fall into our same old ways. At some point, we have to stop lying to ourselves. Finding a soulmate isn't supposed to have this much drama. When soulmates connect, there's no doubt between anyone involved."

Natalia put her hand on the table, and Brett wasted no time extending his to hold and caress it. She didn't budge. "This isn't like before. Everything is so much clearer for me now. My priorities were out of whack. You wanted to maintain a relationship knowing I'd be gone most of the time. You tried to keep things together for us, and I never returned the effort. I understand that completely. I get why you called things off again. And I know to not take it lightly this time."

Natalia pulled her hand back. "I'm not going to sit here and welcome you back. Right now, all I hear is words. I want to see action to back up these words. Show me the changes you're claiming to have made, and we'll see how that goes."

Brett leaned back with a wide grin. "Thank you. That's all I want is a chance. A *final* chance. If I mess this up again, then maybe I don't deserve you, after all."

"I'll be real with you. Right now, I'm focused on finding a job —a career. That's my top priority. I'm not going to take away any attention from that."

Brett nodded. "I totally get it. I'm happy to help."

"No. I don't need an assistant. I can handle the job search myself. But, thank you."

That deflated Brett, but he persisted. "Fair. I'll be here to help you blow off any steam. If you want to go to a movie, or walk around the mall, just call me. I'll be there. But I'm not going to wait for that, either. I'll be reaching out to you. Hopefully, I can make you smile once a day. That's my goal."

Natalia couldn't help but grin. Not all of her feelings for Brett had vanished. He *was* an important part of her life, and she could never discount that. If he really put in the work to rekindle their relationship, she wouldn't stop him. Right now, she didn't know how she'd respond if things progressed back to a meaningful place.

Single life afforded new opportunities, and going back to Brett seemed like that common definition of insanity people liked to use.

This would be our fourth time trying to get things right. Will anything actually be different?

People *did* change. She had heard stories of couples who tried multiple times to get on the same page, to then see the effort result in a lifelong marriage and happiness. Despite her skepticism, she couldn't dismiss Brett so effortlessly.

They had a past and didn't need to go through the early phases of dating. A foundation was already in place, and this time could be different. They could focus on diving deeper into their bond. What really made it tick? What made it keep faltering? They could find answers that elevated their connection to new heights. And just maybe a different future.

"Okay," Natalia said. "Let's start over."

"Really?" Brett leaned forward, smacking the table with both hands.

Natalia raised a hand. "That doesn't mean we're back together. It just means we're starting new. *Show* me how you've changed."

"Consider it done."

Natalia checked her phone. The thirty minutes had passed in a hurry. "I need to get going—have more jobs to apply to."

Brett jumped out of his seat. "Let me walk you to your car."

He hurried to get in front of Natalia, bumping into an empty chair as he raced to open the door for her.

Always a klutz, Natalia thought, touched by the gesture.

"Thank you," she said, passing through the open door. Once she stepped all the way out, Brett rushed to Natalia's car and opened that door, waiting patiently for her to get settled into the driver's seat. He leaned into the open doorway.

"I know we're starting over," he said. "But I want you to know that I love you. I'm going to do everything I can to make this work between us. You've always been in my heart, and you always will be."

Brett leaned in closer, his face less than ten inches away from Natalia's.

He wants to kiss me. Do I want to?

She left him waiting, forced to make a quick decision that could have a lasting impact. If she kissed him, then they weren't really starting over and would pick up where they left off. If she refused, where did that leave them? Was Brett not truly on board for starting over? Did it even really matter? Starting over was just a phrase. Their past remained and wouldn't be magically erased.

We can't actually start over. We don't get to have the early phase of learning about each other's families, likes, and dislikes. That's all known. Maybe I should kiss him. I need to remember what it feels like.

Brett hadn't moved. He was giving Natalia the space to figure out what she wanted to do. Her lips quivered. Heat prickled her face.

She looked up and locked eyes with Brett, their connection on fire. He must have sensed it, too, because now he leaned closer, and Natalia closed the gap.

Their lips locked, and they held a kiss for five seconds.

When they parted, Brett had a grin he couldn't remove. He shook his head. "Wow," he said. "You're incredible. I'll call you tomorrow?"

Natalia nodded.

Brett closed the door and left her alone in the car. The electricity of the moment had vanished, and Natalia experienced the greatest sense of relief as she turned on her car and pulled out of the parking space.

Her future seemed clearer after that kiss. The kiss revealed everything she had been keeping buried from herself.

When Brett's lips touched hers, she felt absolutely nothing but nostalgia. She could say with confidence that Brett was no longer in her future plans.

As Natalia drove away, all she could think about was Adrian.

CHAPTER *Fifteen*

Natalia went into work Friday morning with a rational mind and plenty of positive energy. The weekend loomed hours away. She had a fashion show tomorrow night with plenty of friends confirmed to be in attendance. Including Adrian.

More importantly, after settling into her customary spot in the first seat along the window for her morning train ride to work, Natalia had called Brett and let him know she would never see him again. Brett had pleaded for her to reconsider, citing the passion he had felt from their kiss last night.

The conversation was more difficult than the prior one they had when she had first called off the relationship. He expressed no anger through their phone call, instead sounding like someone had just killed his dog. His voice had wavered when they hung up, and his weekend was surely ruined.

But when Natalia hung up, she drew a deep breath and welcomed the finality. She gazed out the window and reflected on the relationship that had long been needing a definite ending. Now that it had come, she only felt optimism for the future.

"Look at you, lady," Melissa said when Natalia entered the call center. Denver poked his head up, eyebrows raised as he always did when studying a situation.

"Hey, girl," Natalia replied, tossing her stuff on her desk and immediately circling back to Melissa's desk, throwing Denver and Caroline a warm smile as she passed them by.

"You're glowing this morning," Melissa said. "I take it things went well with Brett? Did you get some?"

Natalia threw her head back and laughed. "No, I didn't get some. But I got so much more."

"Ooh, tell me all about it." Melissa smirked, lowering her glasses for a direct stare down.

"Last night was eye-opening. Brett was the perfect gentleman. Bought me my favorite ice cream. He completely opened up—something he'd never done before. He left it all on the table. Said he wants me back, wants to work on our relationship and put serious effort into it. He shared the struggles he was having with us being mostly long-distance. He's definitely changed."

"Well, that's exciting. Good for you two."

Natalia shook her head. "I'm not done. It was a good conversation. We were on the same page and left the ice cream shop, ready to start over. He walked me to my car, and we kissed right before saying goodbye."

"How romantic."

"That's what I thought, too. Only it wasn't. When he kissed me, I felt nothing. No urge to keep kissing him. No desire to see where things could go. It felt like kissing a wall. There was just no reason for me to ever do it again."

Melissa's eyes bulged. "My goodness, Natalia. How did that even happen? I thought you *wanted* to try things again with Brett?"

Natalia shrugged. "I guess I didn't know what I wanted. I'm glad we kissed, or else I'd probably still be giving Brett another chance. He doesn't need another chance. We've done this dance long enough. I called him on my way here and told him I never wanted to see him again."

"You did *what*?!"

Natalia grinned and nodded her head. "That one kiss told me

everything I needed to know, and that is, I no longer love Brett. I've moved on."

Melissa lowered her head, holding her gaze on Natalia. "And you're sure about that?"

"I am. Never felt so sure, actually. It's time."

"Time, or someone else?"

Melissa winked and Natalia's heart fluttered at the thought of that *someone else*. She felt her face flush and could only hope it wasn't visibly turning red.

"I don't know what you're talking about."

Melissa pushed her glasses back up the bridge of her nose. "Sure you don't. Because the only other guy you've been talking to is that one you *hate*, right?"

"Exactly. Nothing to see." Natalia gave a firm nod, not believing it was convincing.

"Funny. It must be a different hate than what I know. If I hated someone, I'd never take them pizza and Coke, even if they had just gone through a rough breakup. If I hated someone in that situation, I'd probably just sit back and enjoy watching them wallow in their pain. Or maybe I'm just crazy."

"He told you about that?!"

"I may have heard about it, yes." Melissa gave a devilish grin. She was clearly amused at having inside knowledge from both sides of this story.

"Okay, maybe I don't *hate* him, but that doesn't mean anything. Ending things with Brett had nothing to do with Adrian."

"We'll see about that."

Natalia's work phone rang, and she had to abandon the conversation, partially grateful for it.

She spent the rest of the morning avoiding Melissa as best she could, staying at her desk and not standing for any reason. She didn't understand why she felt so embarrassed by everything Melissa had said.

Natalia really *hadn't* ended things with Brett because of

Adrian. They had only shared a quick fling in Vegas. If Adrian had told Natalia that he never wanted to see her again, she *still* would have called off her relationship with Brett.

He had no bearing on her future plans.

So why can I not stop thinking about him?

She couldn't deny that Adrian found his way into her thoughts multiple times each day. At least three times a day, she wanted to send him a text message to see how he was doing. But he needed space, and it's not like he was reaching out to her, either. Still, he had found her visit important enough to tell Melissa about it.

Surely he had mentioned something about his stance on Natalia to Melissa, but she couldn't just walk up to her and ask. That would show interest.

Natalia struggled through lunchtime and the early afternoon, hitting a mental wall of exhaustion. Too much happening in her life at once could overwhelm her, and the past couple of days had certainly been busy outside of work hours.

She scheduled interviews for next week that she didn't have the energy to prepare for. Lying in bed for the rest of the day sounded most appealing on this lazy Friday afternoon, and she just might do that when she got home.

I wonder what Adrian's doing today, she thought, already shaming herself for allowing him to pop back into her head. He had the day off, as scheduled, and something about his vacant seat behind her all day made her feel empty.

They didn't need any romantic involvement for her to have that longing to spend time with a new friend. They connected on a level she wanted to lean more into, and every day they weren't at the office together was time wasted in pursuing that opportunity.

Is he thinking about me the way I am about him? Or maybe I haven't even entered his thoughts today. Does he think it's still inappropriate to talk with me outside of this stadium? What if his ex stopped by and they're working things out?

The thought shot pain into her psyche.

I need to worry about something else.

Natalia rummaged through the stack of activity books on her desk, and found a bundle of sudoku puzzles she had been putting off, working on them until the end of her shift at five.

She bolted out of the call center when it came time, rushing to avoid another barrage of questions from Melissa. She made it out of the building in record time and started her walk to the light rail station.

Ten minutes later, as Natalia waited for her train to arrive, her cell phone rang. Her heart skipped a beat when she read the name on the screen.

It was Adrian.

CHAPTER *Sixteen*

"HELLO?" Natalia answered, exaggerating her joy so Adrian could hear it through the phone. She sat on the train that would take her home, earning a few side-eyed glances from those sitting near her.

"Hey." His response was nowhere near her level of energy, all the butterflies instantly draining from Natalia's stomach, replaced by a gnawing that would eat at her for the rest of the night.

"Hey back," she said, keeping a close eye on the sidewalk ahead of her. "Is everything okay?"

"Yeah, I'm fine. Just been a quiet day. Went and bought a basketball. That's going to be my new hobby, at least to start. There's a park across the street with a court. I'm going to play every day for at least thirty minutes. I'll get into shape, and just maybe I can become a respectable shooter."

He explained all this like he was reading off a checklist, no emotion in his voice.

"That's great. I used to play basketball—think I mentioned that in Vegas."

She wanted to see if mentioning their magical week together would spark any sort of emotional response from Adrian.

It didn't.

"That's right."

"Are you sure you're okay? You sound completely out of it."

"I talked with Melissa earlier today."

Shit.

"Oh?" Natalia's heart sunk. She already knew what this call was about, but she needed to play it off. "I talked with her this morning for a bit. Didn't see her much after that."

"Yeah. She's been checking on me ever since the breakup. She told me something interesting, though."

She better not have, Natalia thought, her heart now thumping violently.

"Oh?" she asked, no faith she was sounding under control.

"Yeah, she told me you went out with your ex last night. And that you two kissed."

Natalia remained silent, unsure what to say. For starters, none of this should have mattered to Adrian. They weren't dating. They were friends who shared a week together in a different state. Natalia was free to date and kiss whoever she wanted, as was Adrian.

"Is that true, Natalia?" he asked again after receiving no response.

"Yes, it is." A nervous adrenaline flowed through Natalia's legs.

Now Adrian fell silent, only his breathing audible through the phone.

"Is that a problem?" Natalia asked.

"Not a problem. Not at all." Adrian sounded bothered, but she wasn't sure at which part of this matter. "I was just surprised to hear that because of how adamant you were in Vegas about never seeing him again. I guess I just want to make sure you're okay. If things went well, which it sounds like they did if you kissed him, then that's great for you. You did me a favor earlier this week, and now I want to return the favor by checking on you."

"Well, that's really nice of you. I don't know what to say. I *did* kiss Brett last night, but—" Her brief burst of relief was immediately wiped away when Adrian cut her off.

"But nothing. It's none of my business. If this is what you really want, then I'm happy for you. That said, I don't think it's appropriate for me to go to your show tomorrow night."

"Wait. Why?" Natalia asked, all the joy rushing out of her body. Her emotions were swinging in every direction.

"Look, we have a weird past, even if it's all new. You're trying to work things out with your ex. I'm trying to figure out what to do with my life. If I show up there tomorrow, what does that mean?"

"It means we're friends," she said with some vigor. "And I'm *not* trying to work things out with my ex. Far from it."

"Well, that's not what it sounds like. I judge people on their actions, not their words. I think it's best if I hang back while you get things sorted out."

"Adrian, listen to me," she raised her voice, drawing the attention of others sitting nearby. "There is *nothing* to sort out. He's not even going to be there tomorrow night. I never told him about it. I invited *you*."

"That may be true, but I'm still not comfortable. Things can get complicated. Messy. I just don't need that right now, and neither do you. We've both shared our goals for the future, and that's all we should be focused on."

"I invited you as a friend." Natalia balled a fist, her fingernails digging into her palm as frustration mounted. "That's all. Nothing needs to be complicated. I have your ticket with me today."

"Well, I suggest you offer it to someone else. I'm not going. This should not distract you from your show. I wish you the best of luck, and I can't wait to hear all about it on Monday." He spoke in a rushed tone, and she sensed his urgency to get off the phone as soon as possible.

"Adrian, seriously?! You're misunderstanding all of this. You're not even letting me explain."

"I need to go," he said. "Sorry, but we'll talk later, okay?"

Natalia gritted her teeth. "Fine. Bye."

She hung up, her gut swirling with stress. She *wanted* Adrian there tomorrow, and now that wasn't happening, all because Melissa blabbered about what had happened with her meaningless kiss last night.

I can't tell her anything ever again if this is what happens. So messed up. I thought she was a friend who could keep my secrets.

Natalia clenched her jaw as the train arrived and she shuffled onto it, taking the first seat along the window.

As she gazed at the world outside, she couldn't help but find the irony of how her day had started on the train with a phone call that had been an amazing start to the day—to a new chapter in her life. And now it ended on the same train, her mood suddenly in shambles.

Why do I feel like this? He doesn't owe me anything. If he doesn't want to be there, that's his problem. He's lying to himself because when I invited him, he said he wanted to try new things. This was his chance, and he doesn't really want that. Maybe he should look at his own actions instead of listening to his words.

The train departed the station, and for the first time since before they had left for Vegas, her hate for Adrian had returned.

CHAPTER Seventeen

WHEN JEROME WALKED through the door at seven o'clock, he found Adrian pacing circles around their living room. His hair was a frazzled mess, as if he had been trying to pull it out all day.

"Hey, dude," Jerome said. Best friends since high school, they had been living together for the past three years. "What's wrong with you?"

Adrian laughed harshly. "What's wrong with *me*? What's wrong with women?"

Jerome noticed a bottle of rum in Adrian's hand, only a quarter full. He was fairly certain that same bottle was unopened as of last night. "What happened?"

Jerome worked as a manager at Qdoba, and had brought home a bag of chips and queso, which he placed on the table along with his keys.

"Okay, let me tell you something," Adrian said, spinning around and falling into the recliner. "I like Natalia. Before you get on my case, no, I didn't leave Barbara for Natalia. But Natalia showed me a different side of myself in Vegas. Exploring that other side of me is why I ended up leaving Barbara. Does that make sense?"

"Sure," Jerome said, taking a seat on the couch, settling in for a rant.

Adrian lay on the couch like a patient in a therapist's office, staring and talking to the ceiling. "I never wanted to hurt Barbara, but I had to make a change, you know? It wasn't fair to either of us to stay together if one of us—me—wasn't all in."

"So what's the issue?" Jerome asked. "Why have you drunk an entire bottle of rum?"

Adrian snorted. "I haven't had the *entire* bottle. Not yet."

Jerome had seen Adrian suffering plenty in the days following the breakup. He supposed whatever helped numb the pain was okay for this type of scenario. He'd bounce back and be himself in no time. "That's beside the point. Tell me what's up. How can I help?"

Adrian had always been there for Jerome, ever since high school. He was a steady sounding board and had helped him through his share of rough breakups. Now, Adrian needed to lean on his friend to get through this difficult time.

"I'm not sure you can help too much," Adrian continued, bobbing his head side to side like he was trying to get comfortable. "You haven't even met Natalia, so it's not like you can give me insight into what she's thinking. She had invited me to go to this fashion show she's modeling in. I was totally down. But I just found out today that she went out with her ex last night. They even kissed. Now, don't get me wrong, she has the right to do that. But why play games with me? If she wants to go back with that guy, then go back to him. Don't drag me along for the ride and keep sending mixed signals."

"You know it was for sure her ex? Who told you this?"

"Melissa from work. I guess Natalia told her what happened."

"Hmmm." Jerome stroked his chin. "And you're sure it's credible?"

"Why wouldn't it be? Melissa has no reason to make this stuff up."

"I'm not saying it's made up. But you remember playing that

game as a kid—telephone. Things get changed the more you have different people involved. Have you already talked to Natalia about it?"

"I called her and told her I won't be going to the fashion show. I don't need to put myself through that. Go there for what, to support my friend when she just wants to see her ex? I don't need that."

"Look, you're right about me not knowing any of these people involved, and maybe that's for the best. I don't have any bias. It sounds to me like you're being unfair."

Adrian scoffed, jumping to his feet and pointing a wavering finger at Jerome. "*I'm* the one being unfair?! Bull. I'm doing the right thing, even though it's hard."

Jerome laughed back. "Hard? You're not giving up anything. First off, you don't even know the full story because it was relayed to you. Why did she go out with her ex? Did *he* kiss *her*, or vice versa? Because that makes a difference. Second, you think you're proving a point by telling her off, but you're only killing your own chances. *She* invited *you*. It shouldn't matter who else is or isn't there. You're only making yourself look like a fool, especially because you didn't give her the chance to explain her side of the story. Did she sound upset when you told her you weren't going?"

Adrian nodded. "More disappointed, I'd say."

"See. Even after all that, she still wants you there. Do you know if she even invited her ex? Because what if he wasn't invited, and you still don't show up? Again, you're only hurting yourself, not her."

Adrian sat down and rubbed his forehead, the alcohol clearly taking his mind for a spin. "She told me she didn't invite him… I need to go, don't I?"

Jerome crossed his arms and nodded. "Yes. Especially if the ex won't be there. There's no reason not to go."

"I can't just call her back and tell her I've changed my mind again," Adrian said. "That would look ridiculous."

"I agree. If you go, you'll need to just show up. Surprise her. It's romantic."

Adrian bobbed his head up and down. "You're right, though. I need to let her tell her side. But I can't just show up on this special night for her and expect her to do that. She's modeling *in* the fashion show. Who knows if I'd even get a chance to speak to her? I don't know how it works. I've never been to one of these things."

"I'm not gonna tell you what to do, but if you want my personal opinion, you're not ready to be dating yet. I've known you and Barbara for longer than you two were dating. You don't just get over something like that after a few weeks."

"Ha!" Adrian let out an exaggerated laugh. "If you only knew."

"What?"

"Barbara's already with someone else."

Jerome cocked his head to the side, saying, *Are you kidding me?* "Impossible."

"I saw it with my own eyes." Adrian stared at the floor, spinning the bottle of rum still clutched in his hand.

"You haven't seen her since you two split."

"That's where you're wrong. It was by total chance. You know I got into the habit of parking in that lot next to the Old Chicago downtown that Barbara works at, and then just walk to campus from there?"

"Right."

"Well, just the other day my morning class got canceled, so I headed to school later than normal. Barbara never saw me, but when I turned the corner to walk out of the lot, I saw her. And she was holding hands with some bearded guy. Real scruffy looking dude. The outdoorsy type. Complete opposite of me."

"No way." Jerome jumped off the couch.

"I swear on everything." Adrian looked up at Jerome, eyes bloodshot and droopy. "I know it was Barbara. She was walking into the restaurant to start work."

Jerome shook his head. "So that's what this is all about? You're trying to keep up with her? That's a slippery slope, you know that. It's a sure way to end up in a new relationship you don't actually want to be in."

Adrian forced himself to his feet, a bit wobbly. "No, this isn't about keeping up. I'm not gonna lie, it bothered me seeing that. But what can I do about it? *I* called off our relationship. *I* pulled the rug out from under her. Would I have liked it more knowing she was at home crying her eyes out every night? Sure, that makes the whole thing seem more real. But do you know what I really felt when I saw her and that guy? I realized she was in the same situation as me."

Jerome frowned. "Not necessarily. Everyone handles a breakup differently. Some hibernate and don't show their face in public for months. Others immediately go straight to dating new people."

"Or maybe she just realized everything I told her was also true for herself. You know, finding yourself isn't as difficult as it seems. Many people think you have to spend a year alone in the woods, or something crazy like that. But you're always with yourself. You are the one person you can never escape. If we want to get to know ourselves, we just need the silence to listen. And that's what I plan on doing for the next couple of weeks. I need to become in tune with who I am and who I want to be."

"And does that consist of being a complete asshole by blowing off Natalia?"

Adrian paused, looking into the distance. "No. It doesn't."

"That's what I thought. So, what are you going to do about this fashion show situation?"

CHAPTER *Eighteen*

The crowd at the Jet Hotel bustled with excitement. Models and fashion designers furnished the lobby. Lines formed around the bar, pop music and laughter filled the air, and a close circle of Natalia's friends had gathered in a corner of the room while they waited for the show to start.

Natalia had three different outfits to model for her friend Rachel, founder of the up-and-coming Fashion House of Rae Marie.

She came out to greet her friends from all different parts of her life. Friends from middle school, high school, and college, plus a few from the Rockies, including Melissa, who she pulled aside.

"Melissa, what the hell?" she asked.

"Whoa, slow your roll." Melissa blinked rapidly behind her glasses. "What's wrong?"

"You told Adrian about my night out with Brett. I was telling you that as a friend, not to share with everyone."

Melissa smiled. "Look at how much you care. You like Adrian, and you won't admit it."

The response instantly flipped an anger switch for Natalia. "That has nothing to do with this. I'm talking about you and me. I can't share these private parts of my life with you anymore."

The grin left Melissa's face. She placed a caring hand on Natalia's shoulder. "I get that you're upset, but you need to hear me out. *Adrian* asked me about you. Don't you see? I didn't bring you up. We weren't even talking about you, or work. He brought you up out of the blue. *He* was the one thinking about you."

"What are you saying?"

Melissa's grin returned and widened. "I think you know exactly what I'm saying. He's into you. He doesn't even have to say it, but it's becoming clear. I called him to talk about his breakup, and all he wanted to talk about was *you*. Is he coming tonight?"

Natalia shook her head, resentment immediately boiling within. "No. All because he heard about me kissing Brett. Why did you have to tell him that part?"

Shame took over Melissa's face. "I'm so sorry, Natalia. I told him it didn't mean anything, and he sounded fine with that."

"Well, he's *not*. He called me yesterday to tell me he wasn't coming anymore. That he's giving me space to figure things out with Brett... but there's nothing left to figure out—I'm done with him."

Melissa must have heard the rage lurking in Natalia's voice, because she pulled her in for a hug. "I'm sorry. I'll fix it. It's the least I can do. Let me call him and explain."

Natalia shook her head. "Don't worry about it. He'll come back around. It's not like he can avoid me. We sit five feet apart at work."

"Didn't you two avoid each other for an entire year?"

The question sent a sinking feeling into Natalia's gut. They had always sat in such proximity without ever speaking a word. Who was to say Adrian wouldn't come in to work and shun Natalia for this misunderstanding, just like he always had?

"I don't think he'll do that," Natalia said, frowning and not completely believing herself. "This was his idea, not mine. He has no reason to ignore me."

"I wouldn't be so sure. Adrian can absolutely shut himself out from the world."

"Well, maybe he shouldn't be having thoughts about me when he just got out of a long-term relationship. He's clearly not thinking straight if he's taking your word over mine in this whole Brett matter."

"It's not about whose word he's listening to—he didn't even let me finish explaining the entire story. He just heard the part about you kissing your ex. While he seemed okay with it, I know Adrian, and it was probably eating him alive."

"Exactly. Because mentally he's not in a good place right now. Emotionally, too."

Melissa crossed her arms and shook her head. "I'll talk to him next week. Let's give him the weekend to cool off and maybe he'll listen. I'll even take the fall for this. I had no right to share your personal business with him."

"No, you didn't."

"But I can't help myself." Melissa's face lit up with an enthusiastic grin. "You two are just too cute together. I may have gotten carried away trying to play matchmaker."

"I appreciate your intent, but I really don't need help. I don't think Adrian does, either. As of right now, I'm not looking for a relationship, and neither is he. And that's where we are."

"Okay. I got it. What can I do to make it up to you?"

"How about a shot? I'm incredibly stressed and shouldn't be. I'm walking the runway in half an hour."

"Done."

Melissa spun away and went straight for the bar, sneaking her way toward the front of the line, where a couple of hecklers shouted at her for cutting.

"Mind your business," she shouted back. "I'm getting a drink for one of the models. They can't wait!"

Natalia chatted with her other friends while she waited.

"Hey, *mujer*, you look incredible," said her friend Megan,

giving her a quick hug. Megan was her closest friend, their relationship starting back in middle school.

"Thanks, girl," Natalia replied. "You'd better get a good spot. I'm about to head back for my first outfit change."

"Of course. Good luck out there. We'll grab a drink after, okay?" Megan had always been there, no questions asked.

"Deal."

Megan gave her another hug before pushing through the crowd for a closer view of the runway.

Melissa returned with two shot glasses, a childish smile plastered on her face. "I got us tequila. Nothing better to make you forget about your problems."

"Oh, boy," Natalia said, happy to reach out for the shot glass. "Every rough night starts with tequila."

"On the contrary, I'd say every *fun* night starts with tequila."

Natalia threw her head back and laughed. "If you say so. Consider this the last tequila shot for me tonight, though."

"Cheers," Melissa said, raising her shot glass in the air, prompting Natalia to do the same. "To a wonderful night of fashion, and to the future."

Natalia knew what Melissa was implying with that comment and could only smirk as they knocked their shot glasses together. "To the future," she said, and they downed the tequila.

"Okay, girl, you need to get backstage. I'll take pictures of you, okay?"

"Thank you."

Natalia made her rounds, thanking her friends for coming and promising to spend more time with them after the show. The tequila burned her throat, but its instant healing powers remained. One little shot had loosened her up just enough for her confidence to storm back full force.

I need to get my emotions under control. The audience can always tell when a model isn't in the mood.

The pre-show butterflies returned, a sign she was her normal self once more.

I got this.

Walking the runway required confidence, and not just in her appearance. That was only half the battle. Her legs were waxed, makeup and hair already done by the artists backstage. She needed to *feel* sexy for the effect to radiate down the runway. Having Melissa tinker with her love life—or whatever you'd call it—had torn down her confidence. Knowing Adrian wasn't coming, even as a supportive friend, had put a damper on her mood.

It doesn't matter who's not here. Look at everyone who did *show up. That's all that matters. I don't need Adrian. I don't need Brett. My friends are here, and it's going to be a fun night.*

"Okay, see you all after the show," she said to her group.

Natalia was about to pivot away when she saw the line of people herding through the entrance across the room. There were dozens of faces in the crowd, but only one stood out from the horde. Her heart raced as she locked eyes with her newest guest.

Adrian had just entered the building.

CHAPTER *Nineteen*

THE FASHION SHOW passed in a blur, perhaps the most distracted Natalia had ever been while walking the runway and hustling through two outfit changes backstage.

He actually came, she kept thinking over and over. He stood next to Melissa, less than three feet off the runway, where they cheered and hollered each time she strolled out in a new outfit. She could feel his eyes all over her, and that had only fueled her confidence more.

Natalia knew better than to lock eyes with anyone she knew, maintaining an intense focus to stare straight ahead, calculating every single step she took, mentally timing her appearance in front of the audience.

The dynamic of the evening had changed entirely when Adrian walked through that door. Before, she had expected a night full of drinks with her friends to celebrate another successful show. And while that was sure to happen, there would now also be a conversation with Adrian. In private. They needed to have it. She needed to know what the hell was going on.

She wouldn't consider their dispute a fight, but that he still came to support her after heated tensions said a lot about his character.

Still, she would make him wait after the show for putting her emotions through hell and back.

Rachel brought bottles of champagne for the models to enjoy and unwind after the show. They relaxed on a couch backstage, laughing and enjoying each other's company. Rachel, one of the up-and-coming names on the Denver fashion scene, thanked them for all their hard work. She toasted her models for another successful show, unable to keep the smile off her face the entire evening. Her fashion career was on the verge of becoming a full-time gig, allowing her to achieve her lifelong dreams. Natalia would be forever grateful for her friend, who allowed her to join along for the ride.

Natalia hung out for thirty minutes before Megan sent her a text message asking when she would come out.

She finished her champagne, gave Rachel a tight hug, and ventured back out to where most of her friends remained together in the same corner of the room.

"You were incredible, *mujer*!" Megan shouted, throwing her arms around Natalia.

"Thank you," Natalia said, returning the hug. The lobby had become noisy with the static of loud chatter, and she had to press her mouth against Megan's ear to speak. "You're all so wonderful for staying and waiting for me. Sorry it took so long. We had to get changed. Then Rachel wanted us to celebrate with her for a bit."

"Don't sweat it. We've been having drinks and keeping busy, but we're just ready to celebrate with *you*."

A line had formed behind Megan as the rest of Natalia's friends waited their turn to congratulate her. She spent the next twenty minutes greeting and catching up with everyone, scanning the room for Adrian, but not seeing him.

Did he actually leave?

Natalia didn't think he'd do that.

Still, with each passing second she didn't see him, a bloating pit grew in her stomach. Why would he go through the trouble of getting dressed up, driving downtown, and sitting through the show with no intent of speaking to her? She didn't want to leave things how they ended on their last phone call, and surely he didn't want that either.

As her line of friends shrunk and they scattered around the hotel lobby, Adrian slipped into the line just as Natalia was about to be finished. He held a drink in each hand, grinning from cheek to cheek.

Once Natalia finished chatting with her friend Carlos, the two locked eyes, and that flutter in her stomach returned with a vengeance.

"Hey," Adrian said, handing one drink to Natalia. "You were incredible up there."

Natalia smiled. "Thank you. I thought you weren't coming?"

Adrian pursed his lips tightly and nodded. "I'm sorry I said that. My emotions got the best of me. I told you I was going to be here, so I needed to make sure that happened." He shook his head. "I'm sorry for the way I've been acting. It's no excuse, but my mind is all over the place these past few weeks. That doesn't give me the right to treat you so poorly, especially after everything you've done for me. Honestly, you, Melissa, and Jerome have been the only friends here for me through this breakup. You especially."

Natalia was certain she blushed, looking down to let the moment pass. "What's this drink?"

"Hope you don't mind. I saw the long line of people waiting to talk to you, and you had no drink. I took the opportunity to stand in the equally long line at the bar. Got you a vodka Sprite. If I remember correctly, that was your favorite drink in Vegas. Besides the yard-glasses of piña coladas, which they don't serve here."

Natalia laughed. "You remembered correctly. And yes, that's a shame they don't serve those yard drinks everywhere."

Silence lingered between them for a few seconds. Adrian looked around, Natalia stuffed the straw from her drink into her mouth and took long, drawn out sips.

"If you're not too busy," Adrian said. "I'd love to talk with you somewhere more secluded—and quiet. If you need to get back to all of your guests, I totally get it. We can talk another time."

Natalia looked around. Her friends were caught up in conversations. No one was alone. "We can talk now. Want to step outside?"

Now that the fashion show was over, they had cranked the music up another level to set a night club type of ambiance.

Adrian nodded. They pushed through the crowded bar toward the hotel's outside patio, equipped with standing heaters to take the chill off the cool evening.

Only a handful of others were gathered outside, a couple smoking cigarettes. The booming music faded to a dull thumping in the background.

Adrian leaned against the building, smiling to himself. "Seriously, Natalia, you were amazing tonight. Now, I don't know anything at all about fashion shows, but I could tell you've been doing this for a while. You walked down that runway with so much *presence*."

She smiled. "Thank you. But, what did you really want to talk about?" Natalia was done avoiding the elephant in the room.

Adrian took a long drink before replying. "About yesterday. First off, I want to apologize. I had no right to get upset the way I did. I spent all night and this morning reflecting. I'm messed up. You should be able to go out with anyone you want. I guess I felt a little jealous."

"Jealous?"

Adrian shrugged, squirming his body around, as he could not stand still. "The timing is terrible, but I need to get this off my chest. I feel like there is something between us. I'm not even sure what it is, but there's definitely *something*. Call me crazy if I'm the only one feeling that."

Natalia met his eyes, a grin slowly working onto her face as gradually as sap dripping down a tree. She shook her head. "You're not crazy at all. I feel it, too."

"Okay, good." Adrian sighed and was no longer squirming. "Now, I know we can't act on those feelings. I clearly have some work to do on myself—I never want to lash out at you like I did yesterday. I felt awful the rest of the night. Could barely sleep knowing I had probably upset you."

Natalia nudged him playfully in the side with her elbow. "Don't worry about it. I'd have been more upset if you really didn't show up today. But you're here, and that's all that matters to me."

"It was the least I could do to make it up to you."

"So, what are we supposed to do now?"

Adrian looked up at the night sky, a handful of stars twinkling bright enough to be visible through the city's ambient light. "That's what I spent so much time thinking about. I think the best option is for me to take a step back. I need to work through my own problems, and I should probably do that alone."

Natalia reached out and touched Adrian on the arm, the contact arousing the burning tension between them. "You don't *need* to do it alone."

"I know. But I want to. It's how I think best. But don't want you to worry about me. I'm not going through depression or anything like that. There have been rough days, sure, but what I've come to realize is I'm going through a drastic change. We talked about this when you came over. It's been so long since I've been on my own. I don't even know what I enjoy doing. And I can only figure that out myself."

Natalia nodded. "That's fair. So what do you mean by taking a step back? Are you going to ignore me like you used to?"

She grinned while saying this, earning one in return.

"Not like that, but close. I'll be cordial at work, but I really don't want people getting the wrong impression. Melissa puts stuff in my head, and I can't work through all this with that kind of outside influence. I can't see you for a bit, not outside of work. I don't think we should even go to lunch together right now."

The words stabbed Natalia. She wasn't expecting to jump into a relationship or anything, but also didn't anticipate this sort of news.

"We can still be friends," she said. "Friends go to lunch all the time."

Adrian smiled and shook his head. "We're already more than friends. After our week in Vegas, we both know that, and I don't want to jump into anything in my current state of mind. That's not fair to either of us. You just admitted there is *something,* and it's clearly more than friendship."

"But—"

Adrian raised his hand to stop her. "I'm not saying goodbye forever. I want to make that very clear. Our friendship is still important to me. I just need this time and space for myself. And with that, I encourage you to do the same. You're going through stuff, too. Address it and let's see how we both come out on the other end. If we're both happy with ourselves, maybe we can see if our friendship develops into anything more. Or maybe we'll come out completely changed and wanting different things—that's fine, too. But at least we'll know for sure."

Natalia felt like she had already gone through this personal reflection. After calling things off with Brett, the road to her future had become plenty clear. "How long do you think this will be?"

Adrian sighed. "Impossible to say. A few weeks? Months? How does anyone actually know when they've arrived at that moment of realization? Regardless of what happened with Brett the other night, you owe it to yourself to explore your feelings for him. And anyone else, for that matter."

Natalia didn't want to interrupt Adrian by explaining that was exactly what Thursday night's meeting—she refused to call it a date—with Brett was. His speech seemed more directed toward himself than her.

"I'll admit I don't like this," Natalia said, taking a sip of her drink. The ice was melting thanks to her lack of attention toward it. "And I can't wait around for you, either. Not for a long time, at least."

"I know. I understand the risk I'm taking by doing this, but I have faith everything will work out exactly how it should."

"I'm here if you need me. Don't ever hesitate to reach out."

"I'll miss you, and I'll let you know when I'm ready to talk again. I should get going now, though. I don't want to keep you from everyone else."

Part of Natalia *wanted* to be kept from the party, if it meant spending more time with Adrian. "You're sure you don't want to stay for another drink?"

"I'm sure. When I do something, I jump in right away. I'm going back home to figure out the next phase of my life. I'll see you at work?"

Natalia nodded, opening her arms for a hug.

Adrian hugged her back, squeezing her for several seconds before he pulled back and walked away, leaving Natalia to only wonder when she'd get to talk to him again in such an intimate manner.

CHAPTER *Twenty*

TWO WEEKS PASSED since Natalia had spoken to Adrian outside of Coors Field. The calendar flipped to March, kicking baseball's spring training into gear, and making the call center phone lines busy with giddy baseball fans ready for the upcoming season. This helped keep her mind off Adrian, no matter how close he sat.

Thankfully, it was never awkward in the office. He still spoke to her, granted not as much as in February, but certainly more than last year. He made a point of asking how her day was going each time he visited the water cooler.

They'd swap small talk for a couple of minutes each time, but never anything of substance. He didn't share how his journey of finding himself was progressing, and nor did she.

While she hadn't planned on doing it, Natalia took Adrian's words to heart and did spend some time examining her own life. She had arrived at a crossroads of sorts, and took the opportunity to really drill down into her soul.

She had spent the last couple of weekends going out with friends she hadn't seen in a while. Her job hunt continued, even ramped up. Natalia had to step out of the call center multiple times over the past two weeks to complete phone interviews, but none of these ever led to a follow-up, in-person interview.

The constant rejection was taking its toll. Panic hadn't settled in yet, but she could feel it coming around the corner. With that, Natalia expanded her job search beyond Colorado, something she was hesitant to do, but had no other choice if she wanted to move out of her parents' house in the next year.

"Your first job after college is one of the most important you'll have," Denver had told her one day when she vented to him after receiving another rejection.

"How do you figure?"

"It typically sets the tone for your next three jobs. It will be the only job on your resume besides the part-time ones, like the Rockies. I know it's tough, but stay patient. It's worth it to get this right and not just jump at the first opportunity."

Natalia didn't admit it to Denver, but she was nearing the point where she would absolutely accept the first job offer if it was remotely close to working in the engineering field. She hadn't just spent the last six years of her life pursuing a master's degree, only to pass on an opportunity that seemed harder to reach with each passing day.

Natalia felt both lost and free. She even applied for a job listing in Spain, unsure if she would entertain an offer if they made one. Moving to a different country was a terrifying prospect, but why not force herself into a position to decide? It wouldn't be forever. Besides her family, she had no obligations or reason to stay in Denver.

With the day off from work, she shared these feelings with her friend Megan over lunch at a local diner. They sat across from each other in a small booth near the restaurant's entrance.

"You have a new degree and your full life ahead of you," Megan said, taking a sip of lemonade. "Why not just see where life takes you? Moving out of state could be a lot of fun, if it happens. A fresh start in a new city. I've thought about it, too."

Natalia chewed on her bottom lip. "But it's hard, right? To pick up your entire life and leave takes serious courage."

Megan nodded and gave a weak shrug. "It does. But I've met

plenty of people who did just that, and they're forever grateful for the experience. And you know what, most of them eventually moved back home. They brought all that wisdom and built their life on its foundation. Don't let fear hold you back. You can always find an excuse to *not* do something, but why? Is it honestly worth it? The only person you're holding back is yourself."

"I guess that's true." Natalia considered this, thinking of Adrian and his potential opportunity to move to San Diego and work for the Padres. Would he find an excuse to stay? He was also a Denver native with all of his family in town.

He had admitted to not having a future with the Rockies, but his degree and resume would increase the odds of him landing a job with another team. In a sense, he was being forced to move to another state if he wanted to work in professional baseball.

"And what about your love life?" Megan had asked, always quick to bring up the topic. She was a romantic always on the search for "the one" and never hesitated to share her up-and-down adventures with Natalia.

Natalia laughed. "Romance is the furthest thing from my mind right now."

"Is it? Who was that guy at the fashion show? You and him were talking outside for quite a while."

Natalia blushed. "You saw that?"

"We all did. We were wondering when you were going to bring him in to introduce us."

"He's… just a friend."

Megan pinched her lips together and shook her head. "Nice try. I saw the way you were looking at him. The way you lit up when he walked into the hotel. Lie to yourself all you want, but don't lie to me. Now tell me who he is."

It was impossible to lie to a lifelong friend. Few people could read Natalia as well as Megan.

"His name is Adrian. I work with him. He's the guy I went on that Vegas trip with."

"I thought you hated the guy you went on that trip with? Are we talking about the same person?"

Natalia couldn't help but laugh. "Yes, it's the same guy. I hated him for the longest time. He always treated me like I literally didn't exist."

"And that changed?"

"Well, yeah. In Vegas, it was just the two of us in the evenings. Denver and Caroline went to bed early, so we had no choice but to hang out with each other."

"And now you like him?" Megan arched an eyebrow and leaned forward. "I don't know. It seems risky. How well do you actually know the guy if he blew you off for so long?"

"That's the thing. We spent so much time together in Vegas and kept talking once we got back to Denver. I actually feel like I know him really well. And he knows me."

"So, how come you didn't introduce us and he left the show so soon?"

Natalia sighed before explaining the story of Melissa telling Adrian about her night at the ice cream parlor with Brett and the ensuing fight they had. "He just got out of a relationship, too, and is taking some time to himself."

"You buy that?" Megan snickered. "He's probably out picking up girls every weekend."

"I actually doubt that. He's not that kind of guy at all. If he's doing stuff like that, I'd be very surprised." Natalia ran her finger along the edge of her glass of water. Megan was right. Just speaking about Adrian these days sparked a foreign energy within her chest. Now that he was on her mind, she couldn't help but wonder what he was doing at this exact moment.

"You know I'll always support you in whatever you decide," Megan said, her face softening into a caring grin. "But I also need to warn you when to be careful."

"I know. Thank you."

"Besides, he seems nothing at all like your type. He's way under six feet tall."

Natalia threw her head back and laughed. "He is *drastically* different from my type, but maybe that's a good thing. Maybe my type has been the problem all along."

"See, you said it yourself. You have to shake things up from time to time. We're constantly changing, so it's natural for our tastes to change as well."

"You talk about men like they're trays of food."

"Aren't they?" Megan cackled.

But Natalia wasn't laughing. Her outlook on life and romance had been under her own scrutiny for the past couple of weeks. "If it was only that simple. I've learned that people are more complex than what we see. Think about it. In high school and college, it's all about appearance and status. Looking back, that's all so ridiculous. People stick with others like themselves, and that's just no way to see the world. We're all so much more sophisticated than our clothes and job. The only way you can know someone is by talking with them over time. Not even a single sit-down conversation like we're having right now is enough to truly know someone. It's work, and I think that's why so many of us have trouble finding the perfect relationship. We confuse perfection with ease. Strong relationships don't just fall into your lap. Both people involved have to put in the effort to make it sustainable. Like us. We've been friends since middle school. Have you talked with anyone else from our eighth-grade class since then?"

Megan stared blankly at Natalia. "No, I guess I haven't."

"Exactly. *We* put in the effort to keep this friendship going. It's only as strong or weak as we let it be. If we stopped making time to see each other, our friendship would fizzle away like all the others before it."

"We'd never let that happen." A look of genuine concern crept across Megan's face.

"Of course not, because what we have is worth it. Worth carving time out of our busy schedules to sit down and have a meal together. And that same approach needs to apply to dating. People go crazy dating because they understand this at some level, yet it's so hard to find that someone who is worth all the hassle. Or worse, only one half of the relationship will put in the effort."

"That actually makes sense." The concern left Megan's face, a grateful smile taking its place. "Look at you all wise about romance."

Natalia shook her head. "I wish I had all the answers. This is just what I've been thinking through lately. Trying to make sense of my own love life. And you're absolutely right about looking beyond my type. It's the same thing as all these jobs I keep applying for. Nothing is catching on in Denver, so I've expanded my search to include the entire world. Maybe instead of looking for one type of guy, I need to open my mind and see what else is out there."

Megan nodded, taking a sip of lemonade. "I don't know if it was Vegas, graduation, or even this Adrian guy, but you're really thinking at a deep level."

Natalia shrugged. "Maybe it's all three. I don't know. Adrian encouraged me to reflect on my life while he's doing the same thing. And I have been."

"Well, whatever the reason, I'm glad you're doing it."

"You should give it a try. It's hard to know what you want in life if you don't even understand yourself."

"I just might," Megan said, returning her attention to her meal.

Over the next twenty minutes, they finished their lunch, the conversation drifting to much lighter topics, like summer plans.

Just as they were reviewing the check, Natalia's phone rang in her purse. She pulled it out to see Adrian's name on the screen.

"It's him," she said, showing it to Megan.

She grinned. "His ears must be ringing. I think you need to answer that. Don't mind me."

Natalia nodded before answering the phone, both nervous and excited. "Hello?"

"Natalia! Hey!" Adrian said, an energy in his voice she hadn't heard before.

"How are you doing?" she asked, fidgeting with the small clipboard they had brought the bill on.

"Fantastic. How about yourself?"

"I'm great. Just finishing up lunch with a friend."

"Oh, I'm sorry. I won't keep you long. I'm here at work today, and I won a fifty-dollar gift card to Chopper's. Wondering if you might want to come help me spend it all tonight?"

"Tonight?" Natalia looked up to see Megan still grinning, nodding her head.

"Do it," Megan whispered.

"Okay," Natalia said. "Tonight sounds great. I can make it there by six o'clock. Does that work for you?"

"Sure does. I'll see you there."

They hung up, and Natalia slouched back in her seat, trying to contemplate what just happened.

"Well?" Megan asked, leaning halfway across the table.

"I have a date with Adrian tonight." Natalia tried to keep a grin off her face, but found it impossible. "I don't even know what to think."

Megan smiled back and grabbed Natalia's hand. "There's nothing to think about. Go out and have a wonderful time. Just enjoy the moment and see where the night takes you."

CHAPTER
Twenty-One

MARCH TYPICALLY BROUGHT plenty of snow in Denver, yet the night was a warm one, almost with a summer-like vibe as families strolled down the sidewalk, walking their dogs and kids beneath the trees showing first signs of green life on their bare branches.

Chopper's was a sports bar hidden within the residential area of Denver's Cherry Creek neighborhood. Its clay-colored siding made the building stick out among the surrounding brick homes that had gone up years after Chopper's had first opened its doors, yet it remained a staple and local favorite.

A few minutes before six, Natalia arrived at Chopper's and waited in her parked car for ten minutes as the nerves took a grasp of her mind and body. Adrian had only taken two weeks to supposedly figure out what he wanted moving forward. Was that all it really took? Did he ask her to dinner to let her know his future didn't include her, and that Vegas was all a massive mistake? He had sounded too excited on the phone for that to be the case, but was she not equally overjoyed after her phone call to Brett to tell him the same thing?

That was different. I was in an actual relationship with Brett. Me and Adrian barely have a friendship. Not exactly the same thing. He could be ending all contact with me. But if he wants to explore going further, can I actually date someone I once hated?

Natalia then spotted Adrian's car parked along the curb, four spaces in front of her. The questions still swirled within her car and she forced herself to step out before going down any more mental rabbit holes.

Okay, she thought. *He's in there waiting for me. Stop worrying about will happen and just go with it.*

She drew a deep breath before strolling to the front doors and pulling them open. The bar was packed with the dinner rush, but she easily found Adrian on the left section behind the host stand, waving her over from a booth.

He stood up and gave her a quick hug before she slid into her seat. "Thank you for joining me."

Within that brief exchange, Natalia immediately knew Adrian didn't ask her to dinner to tell her off. His energy radiated with delight.

"Of course, thanks for thinking of me." They settled into the booth across from each other, menus splayed out on the table along with a couple of glasses of water.

"I hope you don't mind," Adrian said, shifting in his seat. "But I ordered us some drinks already. Got your favorite."

"Well, thank you," Natalia replied, that flutter that was becoming so familiar returning to her chest. "You said you have fifty dollars on the gift card?"

"Yeah, won it for selling the most spring training tickets last week. And it's a gift *certificate,* so it has to all be used in one visit. Figured we can have dinner, a couple drinks, and a dessert if you feel up to it."

"Sounds perfect."

Their server dropped off the drinks, and Adrian ordered mozzarella sticks while Natalia took the first sip of her vodka and Sprite.

"So," Natalia said. "If you asked me to dinner, I assume you're done figuring things out with your life."

Adrian grinned, taking a sip of his rum and Coke. "That's fair to say. And thank you for giving me the space over the past couple of weeks. It really is easy to sit down and think through everything, soul search, when there are zero distractions. Outside of talking to people at work, I think I've spoken to my roommate twice over the past couple of weeks. It's truly been an eye-opening experience."

"And what did you find?" Natalia leaned forward.

"Well," Adrian said, folding his hands on the table in front of him. "A good portion of my reflection was about my breakup. Why did it happen? What really was the driving force behind it? Was it my fault, aside from initiating it? It was difficult to come to terms, but the relationship just died. We both turned twenty-one, yet our relationship didn't grow with us, so it got left behind. We were high school sweethearts, but that's all it was ever going to be, I suppose. My next relationship will be much more adult, and I think I'm ready for that."

"I see." Natalia really wanted to ask, *Is that with me?*

"Also, I don't think I'm going to try for that job in San Diego. I want to give one more shot here with the Rockies. Winning this gift certificate was a good start. Over two hundred tickets sold in a week. I just need to buckle down and get serious, and show them I mean business."

"Is that right?" Natalia raised her eyebrows. "Why not even entertain the San Diego job?"

The server brought the plate of mozzarella sticks, Adrian quickly grabbing one to put on his plate. "My life is here. I don't see how I can thrive in a different state. I won't be comfortable. That's just my personality, and I understand that now. I'm not saying I'd *never* do something like that, but I want to focus on what I can control here at home. I've put in so much time with the Rockies—I deserve a shot."

"Well, I wish you the best. If there's anything I can do to help, just let me know."

"Thank you." Adrian took a bite of the deep-fried cheese

before shooting a smile across the table. "Did you take some time to reflect on your life?"

Natalia nodded. "Not as extensively as I'm sure you did, but yes. I'm in a good spot right now."

"That's great to hear. I'm glad you did it."

"Me too. Like I told you, I'm done with Brett. That hasn't changed. But I've also expanded my job search. I've applied to jobs all over the world, just to see what might come of it."

"I see." Adrian sounded rather deflated. "And has anything happened?"

"No calls or anything yet. I still don't know what I'll do if I receive an offer from someone out of town. It would have to be a really sweet deal. I'm not going to just jump at the first job I get—Denver shared his insight with me on that approach."

"Denver is wise."

"That he is."

They fell silent for a moment, giving their server a moment to swoop in and take their orders for dinner. Bacon burgers were apparently on both of their minds, causing them to laugh at their identical orders.

"So, have you talked to your ex?" Natalia asked, studying Adrian for any reaction he might show about the mere mention.

"She called me once. Wanted to see how I was doing. It was nice of her to do that, but the conversation felt so… empty. Weird how quickly we became two strangers—at least, that's what it felt like to me."

Natalia gave a slow nod. "I know what you mean. It wasn't too different for me. I guess people will always come and go through our lives, and we just have to enjoy whatever they provide while they're in it."

"That's deep." Adrian tossed his hands up. "Life is a mystery. We can sit here and dwell on all the people who have touched our lives, but there's no point in doing that."

"I agree. We can only look forward and appreciate the experiences that shape us into who we are."

Maybe Natalia had reflected more than she realized over the past couple of weeks. Hearing her own words, she realized that she definitely had a new outlook on life.

Their burgers arrived five minutes later, and they both jumped in without hesitation, the conversation taking its first break since she had arrived. They watched basketball on the several TVs hanging around the bar, swapping small talk in between bites.

Once they finished, Adrian leaned forward, crossing his arms on the table. "I've had a great time tonight. I enjoy talking to you. It feels like there's no pressure and I can be myself."

Natalia smiled, fighting off a blush. "Me too."

"I'm having a poker night next weekend at my apartment. I'd love for you to come if you're free. There will be a few people from the call center there, too."

Natalia chuckled. "You and your poker. What night?"

"Friday, after work."

"I'll be there. Hope you're ready for me to take all your money."

Adrian threw his head back and laughed. "You tell yourself that. I won my first real tournament in Vegas, or did you forget? I bought us some drinks with those winnings."

"Oh, I know. I just have a way of getting into people's heads. You'll see."

They locked eyes. That electricity had returned so suddenly, so overwhelmingly, Natalia thought it might push her to leap over the table. She wanted him and thought maybe he felt the same.

"Well, I wish you luck," he finally said, blushing.

Oh, he definitely feels the same.

"Shall we order some dessert?" Natalia asked, hoping to ease the intensity.

Adrian leaned back, the tension lingering but cooling off a little. "Yes. I saw that double chocolate cake with a scoop of vanilla ice cream. Please tell me that's something you'd like."

Natalia nodded.

"Of course it is," Adrian said. "Because you're incredible."

Natalia's heart skipped at least five beats at the compliment. They ordered dessert. "So I'm coming over next Friday for poker night," Natalia said. "But when will we get to do something like this again?"

"What, dinner? I can do that any time. I mean, we work together. It's no issue to grab a bite downtown after work."

The date tonight had gone well enough to warrant a second date, and she found herself eager to know when that would be.

The poker night would be fun and all, but nowhere near the level of privacy or intimacy she hoped for. Adrian may only be weeks removed from his long-term relationship, but he seemed in a sound mental space. He had confidence, no more self-loathing, and was excited about the future.

"Well, that sounds great," she said, unable to help her fingers twirling her hair. "We should plan for a night out soon."

Their dessert arrived. A towering three-layer chocolate cake with two spoons sticking out of the mound of vanilla ice cream.

"Death by chocolate," Adrian said, cackling at himself. His green eyes bulged at the colossal dessert, sizing it up to see if he could actually overthrow the beast made of chocolate.

They both chipped away over the next fifteen minutes, leaving nothing but a couple of bites of cake swimming in the melted remains of ice cream.

"You should've told me I needed my stretchy pants tonight," Natalia said, leaning back in the booth, Adrian doing the same.

He shook his head. "I knew we were going to feast, but I didn't know dinner would end like *that*. Absolutely fantastic."

Their server dropped off the check, and Adrian paid with the gift certificate, leaving some cash for a tip.

"Think I'm ready for bed after that meal," Natalia said, standing up from the booth and stretching her arms high above her head.

"Same. Let me walk you to your car."

Adrian hurried around the table, gently grabbing Natalia's arm as they exited the restaurant.

They welcomed the cool evening air after sitting in the stuffy restaurant for the past hour. They strolled to Natalia's car, stopping at the door.

"I had so much fun," she said, staring deep into Adrian's eyes. "Thank you again for inviting me."

His gaze was locked onto her. She thought it looked as if he was trying to get lost in her soul. "There's no one else I'd rather have dinner with. We'll definitely do it again."

Adrian grinned, looking down at his shoes before meeting Natalia's stare again.

She wanted to pull him in and kiss him, but still didn't know if it was too soon. All signs suggested it would have been totally fine. The tension was mutual. But not understanding entirely where Adrian was mentally, she needed him to make the first move. Natalia was ready for anything he might throw her way.

"Well, I guess this is good night," Adrian said. "See you at work?"

The words deflated Natalia, but that brief sorrow quickly vanished when Adrian reached out and wrapped her in a tight hug. She felt his heart hammering against her chest, his arms tense around her back. The skin of his cheek rubbed against her neck, and she leaned into it, wanting to feel more.

He pulled back just enough to plant a kiss on her cheek, his hands releasing their grip from her back and gliding along her arms where he held both of her hands in his. "Good night. Call me when you get home?"

Natalia nodded, her mouth turning to cotton while her legs grew weak. Adrian smiled one more time before letting her hands go and starting toward his car.

Natalia forced herself into her driver's seat and needed a minute to gather herself. Her soul was on fire.

CHAPTER
Twenty-Two

THE FOLLOWING FRIDAY, half of the call center staff packed up their things at the end of the workday and headed for Adrian's apartment. The days were growing busier as baseball's opening day loomed only two weeks away, and an evening of gambling, drinks, and good company was just what everyone needed.

Spirits were high throughout the day, knowing fun awaited at the end. Natalia was nervous, however. Things with Adrian were escalating, albeit gradually, and she didn't know how it was all being perceived by their coworkers. She hadn't told Melissa about the dinner Adrian had invited her to the prior week, and didn't know if Adrian had mentioned anything.

At work, they had no choice but to act professionally. Their conversations were broad, and they had only gone to lunch once together during the week, part of a group with three others. Adrian and Natalia were sure to keep a distance during the walk to the restaurant, but still somehow ended up sitting next to each other, where they played a game of footsie underneath the table.

Tonight, however, would bring an entirely new dynamic to their ever-complicating situation. Not only would they be outside of work, they would be inside of Adrian's apartment. No need for professionalism—everyone would be their regular selves. The mood would be light thanks to the laid back atmosphere, and who knew where the liquor might lead the conversations.

Natalia also viewed the evening as an important test for them both. Working together was one thing, but interacting among their friends in a unique setting would peel back another layer as they learned about each other. Adrian had the advantage as the host. He'd surely be running around making sure everyone was having a good time. As the host, he'd also have the opportunity to see how Natalia mingled with *his* friends.

If romance was simply a lighter version of war, Natalia was bracing to cross enemy lines. But she came prepared. While a majority of their coworkers would show up to Adrian's apartment in their same clothes from work, Natalia had brought a different outfit to change into.

When she parked at his apartment complex, she found the lot already full of familiar vehicles. Her outfit change had given everyone else a head start, but it would all be worth it. Her arms shook as she strolled up to the door and knocked, Melissa quick to swing it open with a wide smile on her face.

"Melissa? I thought you weren't coming tonight?"

"I know," she said, giggling while taking a sip from a red Solo cup. "Denver talked me into it. Said I need to come over and blow off some steam, even if I'm not playing poker. Come in!"

Melissa stepped back and let Natalia enter. There were eight people in the apartment, not counting herself. Six were from the call center, plus two other guys who must have been Adrian's friends. Denver and Caroline sat at the poker table, sipping from cans of beer.

"Where are we putting our jackets?" Natalia asked, slipping hers off.

"Whoa," Melissa said, pretending to tumble backwards. "Didn't realize the girls were coming out to play poker tonight, too. Do they have to pay their own buy-in?" She cackled with laughter, taking Natalia's jacket, and tossing it through the open door of Adrian's bedroom right next to them. "We're just stacking them on Adrian's bed."

"I see. Where is he, by the way?"

On cue, Adrian stepped out of his bedroom, hands held high. "You really need to give a warning before you just throw jackets in my room. That could have clipped me across the face."

"That was all Melissa," Natalia said.

Adrian hadn't realized Natalia had even entered the apartment, coming to an abrupt stop where his eyes looked her up and down twice. "Natalia! Hi. You look… great."

He lunged forward and gave her a brief hug.

"Thank you. Thought I'd get out of my work clothes."

"You certainly did that," Melissa said, laughing at herself before walking away to chat with Denver at the poker table that had been set up in the middle of the living room. The dining room table was being used as the second.

"I think she's a little tipsy already," Adrian said. "She walked in and took a shot right when she got here."

Natalia laughed. "I don't blame her. It's been that kind of week."

"I know what you mean. I'm so glad you could make it tonight. We always have a blast on poker nights."

"Looks like a good crowd." She looked around the living room where everyone was in the midst of a conversation.

"Yeah. Should be a couple of others on their way before we get started. Let me introduce you to my friends."

To her surprised delight, Adrian grabbed Natalia by the wrist and pulled her through the crowd of their coworkers.

"Hey, Natalia," Caroline greeted. Natalia could only give a quick smile in response as she remained tethered to Adrian.

She couldn't help but look over her shoulder to see if anyone else was paying attention—they weren't. Denver sat at the poker table, nursing a drink, and giving a quick nod to Natalia as they passed by and entered the kitchen where the two guys she hadn't recognized stood at the counter filling bowls with chips and salsa.

"This is Jerome and Zach," Adrian said. "My best friends from high school. Jerome is my roommate. Guys, this is Natalia."

They all shook hands. "So nice to meet you, Natalia," Zach said. He looked eerily similar to Tiger Woods, minus the muscles.

"Welcome," Jerome said, clearly fighting the urge to also greet Natalia's cleavage. "If you need anything at all, just let us know."

"Thank you."

Natalia could hear the fakeness in their voices. They definitely knew who she was already, and possibly everything that had happened since the Vegas trip. Just like she had spilled the secrets with Megan, she expected nothing less from Adrian to do the same with his close friends. If anything, it fed her confidence. If he was discussing her with his friends, then he definitely had an interest beyond their up-and-down friendship.

"Are we almost ready to get started?" Adrian asked them. "I don't know where these other guys are, and I'm not waiting all night for them."

"Let's do it," Jerome said.

Adrian shuffled out of the kitchen and returned to the living room where everyone had gathered in different huddles.

"Alright, everyone, we're going to get started," he announced, the room falling silent. "If you're playing, come over to the poker table and we'll draw seats. If you're not, help yourself to the couch and TV, or just hang out. Our games usually last three hours, but people will start getting knocked out after one."

"Probably you," Denver said, earning a round of laughter from everyone in the room.

"You're so funny, Denver," Adrian said with an exaggerated eye roll. "Snacks and pizza are in the kitchen, drinks are on the bar. Please help yourselves to whatever you'd like."

Adrian sat down next to Denver and organized the ten stacks of poker chips on the table while everyone else filled in around them. Adrian spread out ten cards face down and asked everyone to pull one. There were five spades and five hearts to signify which table everyone would be assigned to.

Natalia reached over the table to grab her card and drew the jack of hearts. She saw Adrian had already drawn the ace of hearts.

"Looks like we're at the same table," she said, nudging him with her elbow.

He smiled. "Well, how about that?"

"Hope you're ready for a poker lesson."

"Oh? I didn't realize someone was giving lessons tonight. If I recall from Vegas, you're just a blackjack player."

Natalia scoffed. "That doesn't mean I don't know how to play poker. You just wait and see."

They left the poker table and headed for the dining table where the hearts would sit for the first half of the tournament. Once two players were eliminated, the remaining eight would cram around the poker table and play until one winner was standing.

Natalia sat directly across the table from Adrian, shooting him a glance that made him blush. Filling out their table was Jerome, plus two of their friends from the call center, Jeff Nelson and Ryan Moser.

"Looks like we're at the easy table," Natalia said to Jeff, knowing he took poker just as seriously as Adrian.

"Sounds about right," Jeff said. "I taught Adrian how to play, so it's not like he can get past me."

"The grasshopper will become the master," Adrian said, his tone serious and focused. "I think we can knock out Moser and Jerome and be on our way to the final table."

"I'm just here to drink," Ryan said.

"Cheers to that," Jerome said, tapping his beer can against Ryan's.

Adrian stood up. "Alright, everyone, the timer is starting now. Good luck!"

And with that, the poker game began.

Natalia was no expert on the game, but she knew enough to hold her own, especially in a low-stakes house game like this one.

Adrian had advised her it was rather easy to wait out most opponents and let them make their own mistakes on the path to elimination.

Identify the players who are just there for fun. His words echoed in her mind.

That would be Ryan and Jerome at this table. Since they didn't have a true interest in winning—or simply sitting at the table for three hours—they would likely make aggressive plays that made little sense.

And that's exactly what happened.

After thirty minutes, Moser had lost all of his chips, shrugged his heavy shoulders, and went to grab another beer from the fridge before joining Melissa on the couch. Fifteen minutes later, Jerome was right next to them.

"Looks like that all played out how I imagined," Jeff said with a chuckle. "Thanks for the donations, guys!"

Jerome raised his beer can from across the room in acknowledgment.

Adrian had pulled out his cell phone while they waited for the other table to finish their current hand so they could join as one. Seconds later, Natalia's phone buzzed in her pocket.

She pulled it out to find a text message from Adrian.

Did you wear that shirt to distract me?

She grinned.

Is it working?

Never...

We'll see about that. The night is young.

Adrian stood up, grinning from cheek to cheek, his eyes all over Natalia.

After a ten-minute break where everyone took a moment to grab more snacks and use the restroom, the final eight players convened at the poker table. Natalia was seated two spots down from Adrian, with Denver in between them.

"It's a Vegas reunion," Denver said.

"Yeah, how was that trip?" Jeff asked.

Natalia's heart jumped. She didn't know why it made her so nervous. Did Denver or Caroline know something? Both were sitting in the room, and Denver wasn't exactly the kind of guy to be discreet about it.

"I won my first tournament," Adrian said abruptly, likely having the same anxiety. He glanced Natalia's direction, but she didn't want it to seem awkward, so kept her gaze on Jeff.

"You don't say? That's awesome, man."

"Yeah it was," Natalia added. "This guy kept buying us drinks all week because of it."

"I didn't get any drinks," Denver said. "And I took you on the trip. What's that about?"

"Oh, Denver," Adrian said. "I tried to buy you drinks, but you were always at a blackjack table and told me to not worry about it."

"Oh yeah," Denver said with a chuckle. "Free drinks while you play. Must have been drunk the whole time."

"Sounds like you all had a good time," Jeff said.

He had no suspicion in his voice, no suggestion he had any knowledge of what had really happened between her and Adrian.

I'm being paranoid. Melissa is the only one who knows anything.

Even though her trust in Melissa was on thin ice, she couldn't discredit her ability to keep the secret between the three of them.

The poker game resumed, and after fifteen minutes, so did the text messages.

Natalia's chips had dwindled after losing a big pot when her three-of-a-kind was destroyed by a full house. She texted Adrian.

I'll be out soon. You should join me. Maybe in your bedroom?

She watched across the table as Adrian looked down to his lap where he kept his cell phone. He did a double take before whipping his gaze up to her, cheeks flushing a light shade of pink. Natalia pursed her lips in a conniving smile.

Adrian returned his attention to his phone and responded.

Can't just lose on purpose. They'll know.

Then win already.

Natalia replied, with a winking emoji.

"I'm all in," Natalia announced when her turn came around. She hadn't even looked at her cards before deciding, and was surprised to see a jack and ten, not a terrible hand to put her tournament at stake.

They folded around to Jeff, who announced he'd call the all-in. Then it was Adrian's turn. He paused in silence, folding his hands in front of his mouth as he stared at both Jeff's and Natalia's stacks of chips. The table fell silent, expecting serious action.

Adrian caved to the pressure. "I'm all in."

Jeff leaned back in his seat and stared at Adrian with a puzzled look, crossing his arms as it was back to him to decide if he wanted to call for even more chips and potentially knock out two players in one hand. "Queens? Jacks?" he asked, rubbing his forehead in frustration. "Okay, I'll call."

Jeff was the chip leader so far and had enough to cover both bets. Winning the hand would solidify his odds of winning the whole tournament.

"Let's see 'em," Denver said, and all three players flipped over their cards before the rest of the hand was dealt.

Natalia showed her jack and ten. Adrian indeed had a pair of queens. Jeff had an ace and king.

"Talk about an action hand," Jeff said, laughing as he stood up and crossed his arms. He was essentially in a coin flip against Adrian's hand, and had Natalia crushed. They both did.

The shared cards came up with two aces, ending the evening for both Adrian and Natalia, and Jeff pulled in all of their chips to make a mountain of a stack. He giggled with delight as he struggled to stack them in an organized way.

Natalia wished everyone good luck and stepped into Adrian's bedroom, citing the need to use the restroom. No one else had known about the second bathroom tucked away in his room.

"Not my night, I guess," he said, knocking on the table. "Good luck, guys."

He poured himself a drink at the bar before disappearing into his bedroom, sure to leave the door open to not stir up any suspicion. From the living room, no one could see around the corner in his room where it turned into the bathroom, a walk-in closet across from the sink.

Adrian went all the way in and found Natalia standing in front of the closet door, hands on her hips, that same grin still on her face.

"Couldn't have planned that any better," she said, reaching out and grabbing him by the arms, pulling him in toward her. They exchanged hot breath as their faces hovered inches apart for a couple seconds while Natalia reached behind her to turn the knob on the closet door, pulling Adrian inside and closing it silently behind her.

They left the lights off, and she grabbed him by the neck, pulling him to her face to plant a kiss. Adrian offered zero resistance. Two minutes passed before Natalia pulled away, heart pounding at her ribs like a caged animal desperate to get out. They were both panting for breath when Adrian's phone started buzzing.

He gulped before reaching into his pocket and pulling it out, the glow from the screen lighting up the entire closet. She caught a quick glimpse of his clothes hanging on the rack, dozens of ball caps stacked on the shelves above. But more importantly, she saw the flash of his ex's name on the screen just before he tried to hide it.

"I gotta take this," he said, opening the door and stepping back out to the bedroom and speaking into the phone in a hushed tone. "Hey, what's up?"

Natalia stayed in the closet, stunned, as if Adrian had just jammed a knife into her chest. Her adrenaline was already racing from their heated encounter, but it had immediately shifted to one of rage.

What do I do?

She stepped out of the closet and turned on the sink to wash her hands. She needed to at least give the appearance that she had actually gone in there to use the restroom.

Do I just go back out there and act like everything is normal? How do I even act toward Adrian? Why did he do that?

Plenty of other questions shot to the forefront of her mind, but were interrupted when Adrian returned to the bedroom, stuffing his phone into his pants pocket.

"What was that all about?" she asked, refusing to give him the chance to speak first.

"Sorry, I just needed to answer that."

Natalia's mouth hung open, and she shook her head. "I *saw* who it was. Do you think I'm dumb? Do you still have something going on with her?"

"No, no, no. Not at all. It's not like that." Adrian shook his head aggressively. His voice wavered.

He's lying.

"I can't believe you. We were having a moment, and you just blew me off like nothing."

She marched forward, even though he was standing in the doorway to return to the living room.

"Natalia, wait," he whispered. "Let me explain."

"You'd better move before I make a scene," she said through gritted teeth. "Then you can explain to *everyone* what happened."

He stepped aside, looking at the floor with dread and regret ballooning in his stomach.

"I'm going back out there to have a good time with my friends," she said. "You have nothing to say to me for the rest of the night."

Natalia stormed out of the room and left the party an hour later without another word to Adrian.

CHAPTER Twenty-Three

A WEEK PASSED of Natalia shunning Adrian. She remained cordial at work, saying hello and goodbye—only when he initiated it—but nothing else. He had sent her a couple of text messages asking for the opportunity to talk and explain himself. She ignored those messages. He had called one night after dinner time and left a voice mail that he deserved the opportunity to tell his side of the story, and even apologized for handling the phone call so poorly.

After that voice mail, she finally sent him a text message,

I'll let you know when I'm ready to talk.

She had no intention of ever having that conversation. How could he step away from such an intimate moment? Their *most* intimate moment, not counting Vegas. It erased everything that had happened up to that point. For Natalia, that moment in the closet felt like they were the only two people in the world. Apparently, that feeling was *not* reciprocated.

It was all a lie. The dinner. The flirting. The kissing. None of it mattered if he would just drop it in a heartbeat to tend to his ex. All the work Adrian had claimed to have done during his two-week hiatus was a sham. He hadn't improved himself. He hadn't gotten over her. Now Natalia wondered if he had just used those two weeks to try working things out with his ex. Perhaps that effort had failed, which ultimately led him to finally pursuing Natalia. But maybe it had paid off in the long run. If he was actually over her, like he had claimed multiple times, he wouldn't have been so quick to exit that closet.

Natalia had put herself out there, had taken a leap of faith. And for two minutes, it had all seemed worth it. It was a night of gambling for everyone at the party. Natalia went all-in and lost.

I knew it was too soon, she had thought during the drive home after the poker party.

She couldn't even be mad at Adrian. He was the one fresh off a five-year relationship. Of course a month wasn't enough for him to erase all of that from his mind and move on. She probably would've done the same thing. She was mad at herself for believing him and she resented him for misleading her.

Adrian even went through his back channel of having Melissa talk to Natalia, encouraging her to have a civil discussion.

It didn't work.

The tension was only awkward for Adrian and Melissa, who knew what was going on. No one else did, and hadn't realized how much less the two were speaking at work. Natalia didn't care either way. Let him feel uncomfortable. She certainly did when he abandoned her in *his* closet.

As much as she tried to mentally push all this aside, she simply couldn't. Just thinking about the poker party brought a nasty taste to her mouth. Maybe she was embarrassed. Natalia had thought she was onto something with potential. Instead, she was back at square one. Single and on the hunt for the first job in her new career.

She was driving to meet Megan for dinner, needing to vent about recent events, when her phone pinged. At the next red light, Natalia grabbed her phone from the cup holder and checked the alert.

The subject read: *JOB OFFER - ARCADIS*

Her heart stopped beating. This was finally it. She had applied to at least one hundred different companies over the past couple of months, had three dozen phone interviews, and a handful of in-person interviews.

"Arcadis?" She hadn't interviewed with that company in person, so it wasn't ringing a bell. It sounded plenty familiar, but she couldn't remember which firm they were. "Would someone actually offer a job without interviewing in person?"

Natalia opened the email, her heart sinking at the sight of Spanish text. She scrolled to the bottom of the message to see the company's address in Barcelona.

"Oh my God," she whispered, and the light turned green.

She drove off, dropping her phone back in the cup holder, contemplating hundreds of things at once. Was this a sign it was time to leave everything behind? Break out of the funk that had been holding her back in every aspect of life?

A new job waited on the other side of the Atlantic, and with it new people, new culture. New men.

She hurried through traffic, eager to reach dinner and read the email in detail. Natalia rarely drove like a maniac, but now was an exception. She arrived ten minutes later and didn't see Megan's car anywhere in the parking lot of Jus Grill, a family-owned restaurant that served a wide variety of foods.

Her cell phone possessed the weight of her future as she picked it back up and opened the email again. Natalia shook her head as she read it, falling into disbelief.

The company was offering a generous starting salary, a $5,000 signing bonus, $30,000 in moving expenses, and to cover her first two months of rent upon arrival.

"Is this real?" she asked, just as Megan knocked on her car window, startling her back to reality.

Natalia packed her phone into her purse and stepped out, throwing her arms around her friend.

"Hey, *mujer*, how are you?" Megan asked.

"Honestly, all over the place. Let's go inside."

They headed into the restaurant and were seated immediately, Natalia quick to order a vodka and Sprite.

"So, what's going on?" Megan asked, folding her hands over the menu. "You seem distressed."

"I don't know where to even begin. Last week me and Adrian were making out in his closet—"

Megan smacked the table, eyebrows raised. "Excuse me?"

Natalia frowned. "Yeah, things were going well, and we ended up in there. That's not the point. We were having a good time when his phone rang. It was his ex. He hurried out of the closet to answer the call. Just left me in there."

"What?! Did he come back?" Megan's eyes bulged with anticipation.

"Yes. Like a minute later. He apologized, but it didn't matter. The mood was already killed."

"Did he say why?"

"No. And I wasn't in the mood to hear his excuses. Haven't actually spoken to him since."

Megan nodded, eyes falling to the menu every few seconds as she scanned it for the best option. "And it's been a week?"

"Right."

"You plan on talking to him, right?"

Natalia shrugged. "I honestly haven't given it much thought. But something else happened. Just now, actually. I got a job offer."

"That's wonderful! You've been looking for so long now."

Natalia gave a tight grin.

"Wait," Megan said. "Is there a catch?"

"It's in Barcelona."

Megan's jaw dropped. "I, uh, wow. I know you mentioned applying for a job in Spain. But this is really happening? You're going?"

Natalia shrugged. "I don't know. This literally came into my email minutes ago. I guess I have a decision to make. A *big* one. I have no idea how to go about it."

"I don't know what to say… congratulations."

"Thank you."

"I guess my advice would be to weigh both options. Moving to another continent is not something to treat lightly. Your entire life will change. I know you're close with your family—you'll need to have a long conversation with them."

Natalia scrunched her face like she had bitten a sour grape. "I don't know that I should, actually. They'll do everything to keep me here. I think I need to make this decision on my own."

"Okay. Let's think about it logically. The job is obviously not a concern. You'll have a steady income to live off. However, you'll be going to an entirely new place. No friends, no family. Not even an acquaintance. But I don't think that's a concern. You've never had trouble making new friends."

"I can't just find a new family, though."

"Correct." Megan's tone had shifted to one of a high school counselor giving the same advice over and over. "You'd only get to see them on holidays, and on any other trips you plan to come home. This is probably your biggest consideration. I've grown up with your family. I know how close everyone is. Can you really leave that all behind?"

"It's an eight-hour time difference. Even phone calls won't be so straightforward."

"Right." Megan leaned forward. "What are you hoping to get out of this if you go?"

Natalia bobbed her head from side to side to crack her neck. "Well, it would lay the groundwork for the rest of my career. They are a top firm in Spain, so it will look incredible on my resume. Based on the salary they're offering, I'll be able to grow my savings account."

"And how long would you plan on staying there?"

"For a move of this magnitude, I'd say at least three years. At that point, I'll have my money saved to move back and buy a house here. I'll have the job experience to work with any company hiring."

"But what if you meet someone? Are you going to ask him to move back here with you, or would you stay there?"

The question sent a pang into Natalia's chest. That was a real possibility. Three years was plenty of time to meet someone and fall in love all over again. Was she setting herself up for a future heart break? She couldn't possibly state her intent to move back to the U.S. on first dates—that wouldn't be fair to anyone involved. And if her feelings were strong enough, could she just leave her life in the U.S. behind forever? Only coming home for holidays, weddings, and funerals?

"I don't know."

Natalia didn't know what she wanted. What if she hated Spain? She had visited once, but living there would be a unique experience. Six months in, she could have regret, or grow homesick and fall into depression. These were genuine concerns for people who moved to different countries.

"I think you have a lot to figure out still," Megan said. "And I think you need to talk to Adrian."

"The hell I do."

Megan smiled and raised a steady hand toward Natalia. "Hear me out. I've never seen you light up the way you did last time we had lunch. And it was all because you were talking about him. You might be mad at him, and for good reason, but I don't think what he did warrants you to just call everything off. You didn't even give him a chance to explain."

Natalia leaned back and crossed her arms. "Go on."

"Did this same thing not just happen to you? He caught wind of you and Brett and jumped to his own conclusions. All because he didn't let you explain. Now here you are, in the same situation. Has he been trying to get in touch with you during this past week?"

Megan was right. This was exactly how everything had played out when the roles were reversed.

"Yes." Natalia slapped a hand to her face, then rubbed her temples.

"See, he's interested. If he was really back with his ex, he wouldn't be trying to make things right with you. He wouldn't waste his time if he had someone else to turn to. If he's still interested, and if you think even a fraction of yourself is, too, then you need to let him explain what happened that night."

"Okay. I can talk to him." Natalia pursed her lips, unsatisfied with the situation.

"Good. Because with this Spain decision, you need to have a completely clear conscience before deciding. You don't want to go off to Barcelona and keep wondering what if. That will only set you up for failure. Clear up this matter from last week—I'm sure it's not as big a deal as you're making it. Then be direct and put him on the spot. Ask him what he sees happening between the two of you. And be honest with yourself, too. If you feel there is no possibility of a future, then you can cross that off the list of things holding you back."

"Maybe you're onto something."

Megan scoffed. "I know I am. You need to trust me on this. I think you're not admitting it to yourself, but part of you wants to know what can happen with Adrian. Maybe you talk to him and it confirms you really can move on. Maybe not..."

Natalia shook her head, distraught by the conversation. "Let's order some food. My stomach's been all over the place since I got that email. Maybe dinner will help settle it down."

Natalia changed the subject to Megan and the happenings in her life. She couldn't bear to keep listening to the harsh truth her friend was telling her. Natalia had messed up her handling of matters with Adrian. She acted exactly how he had and that wasn't fair, especially from someone who understood the frustration of not being able to explain the situation.

Through the rest of dinner, they didn't talk about Adrian, Spain, or the struggling job hunt. But Natalia knew she wanted to go visit Adrian immediately after.

CHAPTER
Twenty-Four

DINNER RAN MUCH LATER than expected, so Natalia canceled her visit to Adrian's apartment. Instead, she sent him a text message saying she was ready to talk and would love to go to lunch with him tomorrow.

He had responded before Natalia went to sleep.

I look forward to it

The next day at work, Adrian strolled into the office and greeted Natalia at the water cooler.

"Excited for lunch," he said with a cheesy grin. "Where should we go?"

"Breck? My treat."

Adrian's eyes lit up. He loved Breckenridge Brewery across the street from the stadium, always ordering one of their juicy burgers. "Deal."

Natalia spent the rest of the morning trying to focus on crossword puzzles. She couldn't, then tried reading a book.

That proved even more difficult.

Even though it wasn't a formal date, Natalia couldn't help but be overtaken by elation at the thought of lunch with Adrian.

Megan was right—she still had plenty of feelings for him, and she could no longer deny that.

She hoped Adrian's explanation would suffice. She prayed he hadn't gone back to his ex and that the phone call was simply a fluke occurrence.

After four hours that felt more like twenty, noon finally arrived and Adrian stood up from his seat, slipping into his jacket.

She met him in the elevator lobby where he had just pressed the button. The doors opened right away, and they filed in, just the two of them.

"So," Adrian said. "How's it going? I feel like we haven't talked in months."

Natalia smacked him on the arm, hoping it came across as friendly. "It's only been a few days."

She really wanted a read on his mood. Even through serious matters, Adrian had shown he could maintain a light, positive outlook.

He smiled as he rubbed where she had just hit him. "Felt like months. Just saying."

The doors parted, and they passed through the stadium's main lobby to exit the building.

"Things are going fine," she said as they started down the sidewalk. The restaurant was only one block north. "I want to apologize for the way I've been acting. I may have blown things out of proportion."

Adrian didn't respond, leaving them in a silent stroll. Was he thinking of what to say? Figuring out how to best let her down?

Her stomach twisted into dreadful knots with each passing second.

"Thank you," Adrian finally said. "That means a lot. And for what it's worth, you did blow things out of proportion. That said, I'd like to apologize, too, for what I did. Looking back, I can understand your concern for how that all played out."

"So, what happened?" Relief washed over Natalia. "Why did you act like you *needed* to answer that phone call so urgently?"

"You've never been in a long-term relationship like the one I had, right?"

"Nothing like five years, no."

"We may have just been high school sweethearts, or too young, or however people want to downplay it. But five years is a long time. You get to know the family, and not just the parents and siblings. During five years, you meet *everyone*. The extended family who lives out of state and all that. You don't have to be married to develop strong relationships with the family, so a breakup like this has a long, rippling effect. Even my sister had a hard time with this. Her and my ex had grown pretty close, and that all just… stops."

Natalia nodded along. "Okay, where are you going with this? What does this have to do with the phone call the other night?"

Adrian stuffed his hands into his jacket pockets and looked at the ground while he spoke. "Well, it's nothing like what I'm sure you're thinking. We haven't been talking. She texted me a couple of weeks ago to let me know her grandfather was in hospice care. When I saw her calling, I knew right away what it was about. He passed. She was just letting me know that, and I'm sure she wanted to hear some comforting words. She was in a time of need, and I gave her my condolences. That's all the phone call was. She actually invited me to the funeral, but I'm not going. It's tomorrow. That wouldn't be fair for her to see me and rile up those emotions when she's already trying to grieve. I think she'll call me afterward, and I suspect that will be the last time I ever hear from her. She'll move on for good, and will start her new life."

They arrived at the restaurant and were promptly seated at a table for two.

"Wow," Natalia said. "I feel like a jerk."

Adrian reached his hands across the table and grabbed Natalia's. "Don't. You didn't know. It would have taken me ten seconds to explain before answering that phone call, and that would've changed everything. I messed up, I admit. And then you wouldn't let me explain, and it all just snowballed out of control from there."

Her hands sat in his, and she had no intent of moving them. She loved the way they felt. Safe. Honest.

"Can we just move on?" he asked, green eyes sparkling as he stared into her soul.

Natalia thought back to what Megan had suggested. She needed to know Adrian's intentions.

She nodded, giving a gentle squeeze to his hands. "Yes. On that note, what are we moving on to?"

Adrian released her hands and leaned forward, one eyebrow cocked. "What do you mean?"

"Well, what are we doing? Are we dating? Just friends?"

Adrian pursed his lips, staring at the table in deep thought. "I don't know. I haven't really thought about it. Are you wanting to put a label on us already?"

Natalia shook her head. "That's not what I'm saying. I just want to know where you see things, say three months from now?"

Adrian grinned. "It's funny you ask that. I've actually been thinking a lot about the future since you weren't talking to me. I submitted that application to the Padres."

"Oh, did you?" Natalia tried to sound supportive, but was certain her voice came out as shocked instead. Possibly disturbed. That was not the information she was expecting to receive today. Maybe Spain was calling after all.

"I did. But honestly, I don't think I'm going, even if they offer."

"Why not?" Natalia had no idea where this conversation was headed, and that caused her a great deal of anxiety.

Adrian tossed his hands in the air. "This is the sports industry. I have no doubt the Padres are a better team to work for. They treat their employees better. Ownership and upper management don't pretend the lower-level employees are invisible like they do here. If anything, it's probably *more* difficult to move up the ladder when everyone loves their job. There are still only thirty teams in the league. Each with one person calling the shots on building a competitive baseball roster. Things have changed recently, too. All the guys getting hired into baseball operations have degrees from Harvard or Princeton. The game itself has changed to one of data analysis. I don't see where I fit into all of that."

"But this is your dream. You're just going to turn away from it now? You already have a foot in the door, and that's a lot further than most people will ever make it."

Adrian shrugged. "Dreams can change. I've always wanted to write novels. Maybe I'll do that."

Natalia leaned back, growing more confused with each passing word that came out of Adrian's mouth. She had fallen for the man with his dreams and a plan on how to achieve them. If you took away the dream, what did that leave? Could he still apply the same passion to whatever his next endeavor would be? Or would he simply grow comfortable and never try to achieve something great? This lunch had turned into a lot more than burying the hatchet from their last fight.

"Besides," Adrian continued. "I want to stay here in Denver. I can't actually pull the trigger and just move to a different state where I don't know anyone."

Natalia smiled quietly to herself. Should she share the news about Spain? Did it even matter? As tempting as the job offer was, she felt the same as Adrian. It was too big of a leap. She could definitely handle moving out of state, but to an entirely different continent... not quite.

"I know what you mean," she said, and they took a moment to order their lunch from the server who cut in. They both ordered bacon cheeseburgers. Again.

"Anyway," Adrian said afterward. "I needed to get that off my chest. Make myself hear it, you know?"

"Definitely." *Just tell him about Spain—he's opening up.*

"But you asked where I see myself in three months. And honestly, probably in the same boat as you. I'll have just graduated with a business degree and will need to start looking for a new job. I'd love to get off the phones and do something more meaningful. I might finish out the season—not sure I can just walk away from all those free tickets. I've gotten a little too comfortable having that."

But what about you and me? Natalia wanted to scream across the table. "I know what you mean, could be a fun summer with free baseball before entering the real world. Will I get to join you at any games?"

That was her last attempt to force him to address his feelings toward her. If he couldn't take the hint, maybe it really wasn't meant to be.

He grinned. "You can join me at every game if you'd like. I kind of assumed you would."

"Oh? And why is that?"

"Well, we're hanging out, are we not? I don't think we need to label our relationship yet. We're talking, getting to know each other. I guess you could say we're dating, and I'd like to keep doing that… would you?"

Natalia had been applying so much pressure to this conversation that she hadn't realized it had all shifted back to her upon his returning of the question. Her mouth was turning dry, so she took a sip from the cup of water in front of her. "Yes. I'd like that very much."

Adrian's face lit up with delight. "Good. So we'll keep things how they are, spend some time together outside of work, and see where life leads us."

"Deal, but we need to keep it on the down low at work. We don't need rumors or weird stares. We already had enough of that when we got back from Vegas."

Adrian shrugged. "What's the big deal? Plenty of people have dated each other in the call center, or just fool around. Hell, I think it's almost expected when you put so many college kids in the same room for eight hours every day."

Natalia laughed. "Fair point. It's not a matter of hiding the truth. I just don't want all the drama. We're both going to be out of there by the end of the year, so we might as well keep things how they've been. Besides, you never know if an opportunity could still arise for you with the team. I'd hate for there to be a ridiculous reason that ends with you getting passed over."

Adrian nodded. "Okay, done. Good point. Since we're on the same page now, are you doing anything next Friday night?"

"I don't believe so."

"Good. Keep it open. I'm working on something for us to go do."

CHAPTER
Twenty-Five

ADRIAN HAD that next Friday off from work. Over the ten days that had passed since he asked about it, they went out on four different dates. Two dinners, one trip to the aquarium, and one to an arcade bar called The 1up, just a couple blocks down from the stadium.

During all that time, he refused to share what he had planned for the secret date night.

"It could end up being nothing," he had told her. "So I'm not saying until I know for sure. Either way, we'll still go do *something*."

The anticipation grew even heavier as she had to wait at the office all day, wondering what Adrian was doing at home. They had started talking on the phone every night before bed, and even as of Thursday night, Adrian remained tight-lipped about the secret.

She sent him text messages Friday morning, asking how his day was going, but only received a one word response.

Busy.

He had called during her lunch break, informing her that

things were looking good for his planned surprise, and that he'd have a final confirmation by three o'clock. The afternoon passed without another word, and by the time four o'clock rolled around, she sent him another message to check in and he replied right away.

Sorry. I'll meet you at the stadium after work and will drive us to our date.

Just seeing his response sparked an instant flutter in her chest. She had been surprised with flowers and candy in the past, but never an entire date night. It was both nerve-racking and romantic. She had no idea what would happen during the next few hours of her life, and that sensation made her feel so *alive*.

Melissa ventured to the water cooler and filled a cup. "What's that big smile on your face for?" she asked.

Natalia put her phone down. "Nothing. Just read something funny."

"Right. You and Adrian going out tonight?"

Natalia's heart raced. How could Melissa possibly know? "Why do you say that?"

"Haven't you been going out all week?"

Natalia widened her eyes at Melissa and waved her hand to tell her to quiet down. "How do you know that?" she whispered. "Did Adrian tell you?"

Melissa squatted down so only Natalia could hear her. "Girl, no one had to tell me. You two might think you're being sneaky, but you can't help the way you look at each other. Going to lunch together every day, walking out together after work. You both act different when one of you has a day off. Not sad, just like something is missing. So it's true then, you two have been going out?"

Natalia nodded. "But don't tell anyone. We're trying to keep it on the hush."

Melissa pursed her lips and did the old motion of pretending to zip her mouth shut. And she threw away the invisible key for good measure. "I'm so happy for y'all. You two are perfect together. And don't worry, your secret is safe with me."

Melissa patted her on the leg before standing up and returning to her desk.

The final forty-five minutes of the workday dragged for an eternity. Natalia wasted ten minutes trying to guess where Adrian would take her. It was impossible. Denver had hundreds of things to do on any given Friday night. She eventually gave up and simply stared at the clock on her work phone, each minute passing by, one agonizing tick at a time.

About three months later, by Natalia's judgement, five o'clock finally arrived, and she darted out of the call center without so much as a goodbye to anyone else. She hurried to the break room to clock out, and rushed down the stairs to reach the underground tunnel, leaving no chance of getting caught up in a conversation in the elevator, or worse, stuck walking with one of her elderly colleagues.

The parking lot was outside of the center field gates, while the call center was behind home plate. Today was not the time for a casual stroll through the tunnels that smelled of peanuts and the tangy yeast from the stadium's in-house brewery.

Natalia made record time through the tunnels, stepping outside to the parking lot in less than a minute. And there he was, leaning against the front of her RAV4 in a pair of dark jeans and a sky blue t-shirt, a charming grin plastered across his face.

"You ready?" he asked once she reached her car.

"Sure," she said, trying to sound like she hadn't been counting down the milliseconds all day, and doing a horrendous job.

"Good day at work?" He extended his arm and rubbed her shoulder.

"Long day, but not too bad. So, what are we doing? Should I change?"

Natalia had worn a pair of khakis and a gray vest over a white t-shirt.

"You look beautiful, as always. No need to be fancy where we're going. Now, let's go."

He waited for her to toss her backpack into her car before grabbing her hand and leading them to his silver Civic.

The compliment. The hand holding. Natalia was melting inside and couldn't resist wanting more of that feeling.

They got in the car, and Adrian sped out of the lot. She wasn't sure if he did so none of their colleagues would see them together, or if he was just as anxious as her to get to the date.

"We don't have a long drive at all," he said once the stadium was in the rearview. "We're staying downtown, actually."

Traffic was filling the roads with everyone breaking for the weekend. It was the first warm day of the spring—it had hit seventy degrees at lunch time—so crowds of people herded down the sidewalks to pack the bars lining both sides of Blake Street as they headed south.

Natalia shared about the workday while they continued down Blake, eventually merging onto Auraria Parkway. Adrian flicked on the turn signal before entering the parking lot for the Pepsi Center.

"We're going to a Denver Nuggets game?!" Natalia asked.

Adrian grinned. "You mentioned basketball is your favorite sport. I spent all day in a bidding war online for some really incredible seats. But first, we'll head into Blue Sky Grill for dinner."

Natalia gasped. "I'm so *excited,*" she said, unable to wipe the smile off her face.

"Good. It should be a fun night. The Spurs are in town."

"Tim Duncan is my giant teddy bear. Can't wait to see him play."

They parked, climbed from the car, and held hands as they walked to Blue Sky Grill, the restaurant inside the stadium. Over the next hour, they enjoyed drinks and dinner, swapping stories about past basketball games they had attended.

Once they wrapped up, Adrian led them toward their seats.

They entered the section behind the Spurs bench and descended the stairs, getting closer and closer to the court. He finally stopped at a row near the bottom, only two rows behind the Spurs bench.

"Here we are," he said, holding out his arm for Natalia to enter their row.

"Wow," she said, settling into her seat. The players were only feet away, towering giants up close. "I've only sat this close a couple of times. It's really a different game down here."

"I know it. I always get as close as I can when the Bulls come to town. You can hear everything the players are saying. It's like being more involved in the game. Look, we even get service in these seats."

Adrian pointed to the end of the row where a man was taking food and drink orders from other fans.

They hung out in their seats for the next half hour, watching the players warm up before the game eventually tipped off. During the first time out, Adrian leaned over and asked if Natalia was having a good time. She responded by leaning closer to him and planting a kiss on his lips. "I'm having an amazing time."

"Good. You deserve it."

"Say, we need to talk about something." Natalia looked around until settling on Adrian.

"Oh? Is everything okay?" Adrian's eyes narrowed on her, searching for the potential issue.

"Everything is great. Maybe *too* great. It's just that Melissa seemed to know we've been seeing each other."

Adrian shot his hands up. "I haven't said a word."

"I know. She said as much, but also mentioned she could tell something's going on between us."

Adrian leaned back in his seat, slipping his arm around Natalia's shoulders. "And what's wrong with that?"

Natalia sighed. "I just don't want all the call center putting their noses into our business. You know how everyone is."

"So, what, we just need to act like we did before the Vegas trip?"

Natalia laughed. "Doesn't need to be that extreme. Just don't give anyone a reason to think anything is going on. Melissa promised to keep it a secret, but she knows. Let's keep it at that."

Adrian chuckled. "Seriously. Can you imagine if Denver found out? He'd try to take all the credit for setting us up."

"I don't doubt that. Maybe he deserves *some* credit—as does Caroline—but still."

Adrian laughed, pulling Natalia tighter into his one-armed embrace. "It's kind of romantic, don't you think?"

"What? Pretending we're not seeing each other?" Natalia leaned into Adrian, noting how she fit perfectly against his shoulder.

"Not when you put it that way. I meant the secrecy. Sneaking around. I've never done anything like this before."

"Well, hopefully it's not for long. I have a job interview I'm feeling great about next week. Just might be the one."

"And it's here in Denver?"

The way Adrian asked that question made her wonder if he had somehow heard about the offer from Spain, like he was begging her to stay. But he had no way of knowing. He'd never even met Megan before, and she was the only person who knew about that offer.

"Yes, here in Denver."

She watched the relief sweep over his face. He didn't say anything in response, only nodding his approval.

"But you're on board with keeping it a secret?" she asked.

"Of course. As long as I don't have to do it forever, I think I can manage."

Forever?

The word was intimidating in any regard. Definitive. Infinite. But in a romantic sense, it carried so much more weight. His use of the word suggested he had thoughts about Natalia remaining in his life for how long? Certainly not *forever*—that was ludicrous to think after a few weeks of dating. But would it last beyond their employment together at the Rockies? Would seeing each other less weaken the connection they had built?

"Natalia?" he asked, nudging her out of her daydream.

"Sorry, what?"

He was grinning at her, leaning in close enough to kiss again. "I asked if you wanted a drink? He's coming back around to take orders."

"Oh, yes. I'll just have a water."

Natalia felt sick to her stomach all of a sudden. She couldn't help but dwell on his choice of words. He was deliberate with the things that came out of his mouth, so she couldn't chalk it up as some subconscious mistake. If he said it, then he meant it, though he surely didn't mean for her to get consumed by it.

They enjoyed the rest of the game together, laughing and sharing stories, still getting to know each other. Natalia pushed her thoughts aside once she realized Adrian had no plans of getting down on a knee today. She was even disappointed in herself for wasting so much energy on the matter.

When the final buzzer sounded, the Nuggets celebrated a 115-112 victory over the Spurs, and Natalia threw her arms around Adrian. "Thank you so much for tonight. I had such an incredible time."

"You're very welcome. I wouldn't have wanted to share this night with anyone else."

She kissed him again—and couldn't stop doing it. The strings in her heart felt stretched to their capacity. They just might snap any day now.

He kissed her back, and they held each other while the rest of the arena cleared out, taking their time to mosey outside. The temperature had fallen once the sun had set, but the night remained beautiful as they walked to Adrian's car, hands intertwined.

They talked about the excitement of the game once they were in the car and back on the road to Coors Field. The traffic from earlier had vanished in the later hours, and they returned to the stadium five minutes after they broke free of the jammed traffic surrounding the Pepsi Center.

Adrian pulled right next to Natalia's car and parked.

"Thanks again," she said, hanging her head as she gathered some much needed courage.

"Of course. Is something wrong?" Adrian killed the engine to leave them in silence.

Natalia gently shook her head. "Not at all. I've just been thinking."

"About?"

"Us. Tell me if I'm wrong, but I feel like we have something. It's hard to say how serious it is, but I can't deny it's something real. Do you feel it?"

Adrian nodded, a subtle grin touching his lips. "I do. I can't spend enough time with you. I'm already sad I have to say good night and leave you."

"Don't be sad. That's a good feeling. I have it, too. It could be the opposite, and you can't wait for me to get out of the car." She chuckled at herself, but Adrian didn't budge.

"Never."

"If this is going too fast, just tell me. But I'd love for you to come have dinner with my family."

Adrian widened his eyes. "Really?"

"I knew it. Too soon. Forget I said anything."

"Hold on a minute. I didn't say no. I'd love to, actually. I'm just curious how you're going to introduce me, since I'm not your boyfriend."

Natalia smirked. "Well, if you're not my boyfriend, then I'll introduce you as my friend. It's not that big of a deal."

"But isn't meeting your family a big deal? If you're bringing a guy home to meet your parents, that *usually* means things are more serious than being friends. At least that's how I understand our society. In fact, it's one of the ultimate acts of approval people seek before deciding to take the next step with someone."

Natalia desperately wanted to ask Adrian if he *wanted* to be her boyfriend, seeing how much he brought up the topic. But she couldn't. That decision was ultimately up to him, considering he was most recently out of a prior relationship. Despite that, she had no idea how she'd respond to the question of making their dating relationship exclusive.

"Call it whatever you want," she said. "I'm just asking my charming, handsome friend if he'd like to come have dinner with my family. No pressure, and you can totally say no. I won't be offended."

Adrian smiled. "I'll be there. Tell me when."

CHAPTER
Twenty-Six

FOUR DAYS LATER, Adrian sat behind the wheel, driving to the city of Aurora for the first time he could recall. His hands trembled on the steering wheel, nerves flashing throughout his entire body.

Why am I making such a big deal out of this? It's just dinner. It doesn't mean anything.

He had been telling himself this lie all day. Dinner with Natalia's family meant *a lot*. He remembered having dinner at Barbara's house in high school for the first time. No matter the scenario, the parents of someone you're hoping to date always have an intimidation that can't be matched. It was a necessary step, but what might it reveal?

So far, Adrian liked *Natalia*. Putting friends and family members into the mix could make things complicated. If one of Natalia's parents didn't like Adrian, how might that muddy the waters? We're taught from a young age to respect the opinions of our parents, so if one disapproved of who we brought home, did that change the lens through which we viewed that person?

Everything could change after tonight.

It can change for the better, too, Adrian reminded himself.

He pulled out his cell phone and dialed Jerome.

"What's up?" Jerome answered.

"Hey, man, I know you're at work. But I didn't get to talk to you at all this weekend. I'm going somewhere right now."

"Is everything okay?"

"Who knows? I'm going to have dinner with Natalia and her family at their house."

"Oh!" Jerome said, surprised. "Good luck? Dang, man, I don't know what to say."

"I was hoping you did. I can't remember the last time I've felt this nervous. And Aurora is *so* far. It's adding to my torture right now."

"Now that I think about it, I think I've only had to meet a girlfriend's parents once. All the others were from out of state, and their parents didn't live here."

"That's not helping."

Jerome snickered. "Right. Best thing you can do is to be yourself. Don't lie to impress the family. That will only come back to hurt you later. And I mean it. Don't lie about *anything*, even if you think it's completely irrelevant."

"Now *that* sounds like a personal experience."

"Let's just say I ended up on a golf course with an ex's father. And I'd never touched a golf club before that day."

Adrian chuckled. "I need to hear more about this story."

"Another time. But for your dinner tonight. Do you know who's all going to be there? Does she have any siblings?"

"She has a younger sister and brother, and they all live there, so I'm assuming they'll be at dinner."

"That's good. It leaves less time with just the parents. They can't grill you as hard if there are others in the conversation. Besides, you've always been good at connecting with new people, even when you don't want to. Get on the good side of her siblings —which is much easier."

"I suppose. It also increases my chances of saying something wrong."

"You'll be fine. You survived Barbara's dad, and that guy was intense. He might have even liked you toward the end of things."

Adrian giggled. "I'm sure he just *loves* me now."

"If you can get through him, you can handle anyone else."

"I don't know. This is a Latin family. Completely different ballgame. Her mom is Colombian and her dad is Venezuelan."

"So they know where to hide your body if you get out of line. Not a big deal. Just don't get out of line."

Jerome cackled, tickled with himself and his jokes during a stressful time.

"Not helping."

"You're overthinking it. Like you always do. Just go in there and be yourself. Try to make everyone laugh at least once, and you'll be set. I gotta get going, though. Customer just walked in."

"Fine. Talk to you tonight."

"Good luck, man."

They hung up, and Adrian tossed his phone on the passenger seat.

Jerome was right, he was overthinking this. It was just dinner at Natalia's house. Low key. His first time meeting Barbara's parents was the night of their junior-year prom, with dinner at a country club in front of all their rich friends. *That* was nerve-racking.

"Be myself?" Adrian asked his car. "What does that even mean anymore?"

The past month of his life had been a massive transformation. He had a better understanding of what he wanted out of life, but did that translate to who he *was* at his core?

Perhaps it was too soon to take this step in his relationship with Natalia, but he couldn't sit out these opportunities, either. Being with her felt like the right thing to do, and sitting by would only guarantee her eventually finding love from someone else.

Every decision he had made since the Vegas trip was now coming full circle. He had put himself in this situation and it was time to face the reality. He exited the freeway, now ten minutes away from his destination.

His guts bubbled with angst. It was rare to know when your life was about to change forever, but Adrian understood this moment was exactly that.

Just three miles away waited five people ready to make their judgement. Would they like him? Would he fit in? Could they treat him like one of their own? The answers to these very questions would dictate how the coming weeks and months would play out.

"I can do this."

Adrian looked at himself in the rearview while stopped at a red light. He needed the words of encouragement.

First impressions set the stage for everything. Bad ones could be erased over time, but that was more the exception to the rule.

"I should have brought flowers. Dammit."

Flowers for Natalia. For her mom. For her sister. And what about her dad and brother?

He scanned his surroundings, having never driven on this particular road ever before. He passed a pharmacy and saw a grocery store at the next intersection where he needed to turn.

"Candy? Beer? I don't even have enough money for all that."

His mind raced as he approached the intersection, the King Soopers grocery store daring him to pull into the parking lot.

At the last second, he swerved across two lanes and turned in, promptly parking in the first available space. He panted for breath, body filled with adrenaline and tension.

"What am I doing? I can't show up with flowers. That's too much. Desperate. Flowers die in ten days—such a dumb gift."

Be yourself, his inner voice reminded.

The last thing Adrian would do was show up at someone's house with flowers. And he wouldn't start today.

He drew a deep breath before reversing the car and driving back onto the main road, now two minutes away from the Ayala house.

In a rare occurrence, Adrian hit every green light the rest of the way and pulled into the cul-de-sac where he saw Natalia's car parked in front of her house, two other vehicles in the driveway.

He parked next to Natalia's Toyota and killed the engine, giving one last glance to himself in the mirror.

"Okay, this is it. No turning back now."

CHAPTER Twenty-Seven

"EVERYTHING NEEDS TO BE PERFECT," Natalia said, having bounced around the kitchen for the last hour.

"Relax," Natalia's mom, Mariana, said as she tended to the pot of chicken on the stove. "Everything is just right. Besides, I thought it was just a 'friend' coming over, so what's the big deal?"

"Oooh, someone's in love," cackled her brother, Alejandro, the youngest of three siblings. Even as adults, he still poked fun at her like their middle school days when she had first started liking boys.

"Shut up!" Natalia snarled, smacking him in the arm.

"Yep, that's definitely love," he said, rubbing the sore spot and letting out a nervous chuckle.

"I'm *not* in love," Natalia said through gritted teeth. "He really is just a good friend."

Her younger sister, Alicia, shuffled down the stairs, chomping on a piece of gum, and entered the kitchen. "What's all the commotion?"

"We're having dinner for your sister and her friend tonight," Mariana explained, moving from the chicken to the rice cooker on the counter. "And your sister's being a bit of a perfectionist."

"Because she's in looooove," Alejandro teased, swiftly earning another punch to balance out both arms.

"Stop hitting your brother," Mariana snapped from across the room, pointing a sauce-covered ladle at the bickering siblings. "I suggest you three set the table. Dinner's almost ready."

Just hearing those words made Natalia's stomach sink. If dinner was almost ready, then Adrian would soon come knocking on their door. And what awaited when she pulled open that door and he met the people she had spent her entire life with?

Well, a reality check.

No, she wasn't in love, but she couldn't rule out the possibility of using such a delicate word someday. Tonight's dinner would go a long way in deciding just that. The best path forward. If her family adored Adrian, she'd have no excuses for diving all the way into a serious relationship with him. Taking that next step, and just maybe, put a label on their connection.

And if they don't like him?

She tried to not think about such a possibility. It was only dinner. It's not like Adrian was meeting her extended family. Thanksgiving dinner typically had seventy relatives attend, and they were all close. Now *that* would be pressure.

He had to pass this simple test before facing the wolves of Natalia's uncles, aunts, and cousins. Never mind her grandparents, whose portrait on the living room wall gave the intimidating vibes of a couple of Colombian drug lords.

"Adrian is coming over?" Alicia asked, eyes boring into her older sister, her big lips pursed in disappointment for not knowing sooner.

"Stop it," Natalia said in a hushed tone, setting out napkins on the dinner table. Six, instead of the usual five.

"Oh, so you get to hear about him, but not me?" her mom asked, turning away from the stove.

"Yeah," Alicia said. "It's the guy she went to Vegas with. I guess what happens in Vegas *doesn't* stay in Vegas."

They all burst into laughter, except for Natalia. To round out the group, her dad sauntered down the stairs and joined them in the kitchen.

"Long day of work," he said, having changed into a pair of shorts and a tattered t-shirt. "Did I hear Natalia has a new boyfriend?"

Natalia rolled her eyes, sighing. "You guys are the worst. No, Dad, I don't have a boyfriend. Just a friend coming over for dinner."

"Just a friend," he repeated, nodding. "Me and your mom were 'just friends' once."

A knock on the door interrupted their conversation. Natalia was equally grateful and anxious as the blood froze in her veins.

"Your *boyfriend's* here," Alejandro said, smirking.

Natalia shot him a death glare before strolling to the door, hoping it was enough to silence her unpredictable brother.

"Everybody be nice," Mariana said, circling around the kitchen counter to gather with the rest of the family eagerly waiting to meet Adrian. "This is important for Natalia."

At least someone has my back, Natalia thought as she reached for the doorknob and pulled it open.

Adrian stood in the doorway, grinning, with his hands stuffed into his pockets. "Hey."

His voice came out soft and clearly nervous, and that relieved Natalia. His nerves meant she wasn't alone, and also that the evening ahead was just as important to him.

"Come in." Natalia stepped aside and let Adrian enter. Her family gathered in front of the dining table, waiting patiently for their formal introductions.

"Welcome to my home," she said, shuffling backward toward her family. She wanted to pull him by the arm, but her siblings would be all over that if they saw. "This is my mom."

"Nice to meet you," Adrian said, sticking out a hand.

"I'm Mariana. You can call me Mari. And it's very nice to meet you." She took his hand before pulling him in closer. "We hug in this family."

"No worries," Adrian said with an unsteady laugh, returning the hug. "Mine is the same way."

"And this is my dad," Natalia said, continuing down the row.

"Hello, Mr. Ayala."

"No Mr. Ayala," he replied, sticking out a beefy hand. "Call me Leo." They shook hands, Leo patting Adrian on the shoulder before they let go.

"My brother Alejandro and sister Alicia," Natalia said.

"Nice to meet you," Alicia said, a devilish grin touching her lips. "I've heard sooo much about you."

"Good things, I hope," Adrian replied, but his words were lost while Natalia smacked her sister across the back.

"Ignore them," her brother said, stepping forward to shake Adrian's hand. "Adrian and Alejandro. Hopefully, they don't mix us up."

"We actually thought about naming him Adrian at one point," Mari said. "But we decided on Alejandro."

"Both are good names," Adrian said, his voice sounding more like its normal self.

"Are we ready for dinner?" Mari asked, giddily clasping her hands together. "Alicia, why don't you serve drinks for everyone, please?"

They all settled around the table, Adrian taking the seat next to Natalia, facing her father.

"So, how was the drive?" Leo asked. "Where do you live?"

"I'm in Thornton. Wasn't too bad. The only heavy traffic was on 270, but it's always that way."

"You work with Natalia?" Alejandro asked, sliding his large body around the table to take his seat.

"Yeah." Adrian replied as he fidgeted with the silverware on his napkin.

He really is nervous, Natalia thought. *It's almost cute.*

"I'm sorry," Alejandro said with a disappointed shake of the head. "I can't even imagine working with my sister every day."

They both laughed. "She's not so bad," Adrian said. "She's the best partner to have for stuffing envelopes, that's for sure."

Natalia giggled. The conversation was flowing well enough, and no one seemed *too* uncomfortable.

Alicia returned to the table with cups filled with lemonade, Mari following behind with plates full of chicken and rice drowned in tomato sauce. Once everything was passed around, they sat down, said grace, and started eating.

"So," Alicia said after enough awkward silence had passed. "You went to Vegas with Natalia last month, huh?"

"Well, I'd say she came with me," Adrian said. "It was a trip for my twenty-first birthday."

"You just turned twenty-one?" Alicia asked. Adrian nodded as he stuffed a bite of rice into his mouth. "Wow, Natalia. Cradle-robbing much? I just turned twenty-one back in August, so we're basically the same age."

Natalia kicked Alicia under the table, sure to land the blow directly on her sister's shin. She wasn't entirely thrilled about the thought of dating a guy almost three years younger than her, and Alicia so quickly pointing out the fact did her no favors.

"It's not a big deal," Mari said, rolling her eyes at Alicia. "My mom is four years older than my dad. I think once you're out of high school, it doesn't really matter."

"Exactly," Leo said, putting down his fork and taking a sip from his cup of water. "Are you in college, then?"

"Yes," Adrian said. "I'll graduate in May with a business degree."

"Very nice. What do you plan on doing?"

"I don't know yet. I'll probably finish out the season with the Rockies. Hopefully, they'll make the playoffs so I can go to the games. But after that, I'm not sure. I'll find something."

"Well, good luck," Leo said. "We used to run a flower shop

before the recession, so you could say we've gone to business school, in a sense. It isn't easy."

Natalia didn't like the questions, as it felt more like an interrogation. But Adrian didn't seem bothered. And somehow he kept forking food into his mouth through it all.

The rest of dinner passed without a hitch. Leo and Alejandro took a liking to Adrian, badgering him with questions about his favorite sports teams and what type of activities he enjoyed in his free time.

Mari cleared the table and served everyone a bowl of ice cream for dessert.

"I want to hear Adrian's point of view," Alicia said, making direct eye contact with their guest and purposely ignoring her older sister. "Natalia says you're only friends. Is that true?"

Mari smacked Alicia on the back of the head. "That's none of your business."

Alicia only laughed in response, Alejandro grinning next to her as he pretended to shift his focus to the ice cream in front of him.

Adrian laughed, instantly lightening the mood. "It's okay, really. We definitely have a strong friendship that started in Vegas. And right now, we're just seeing where things go. We've gone on a few dates, and I think we've had a good time."

"We have," Natalia said, desperate to wrestle any semblance of control back over this conversation.

"Well, for what it's worth," Alicia said. "I approve."

The words struck Natalia more positively than she had expected. She never knew what her sister would spew at any moment, so she embraced the rare compliment.

"Well, thank you," Adrian said. "I've enjoyed dinner with you all, too."

They sat around the table for the next hour, chatting, diving into Adrian's life. Something he'd say would spark a story from Leo, letting Adrian learn something about Natalia's past.

By the end of the conversation, her family swapped hugs and handshakes before Adrian left—a favorable sign he'd be welcomed back a second time. Natalia walked him to his car parked along the curb, the nerves from earlier completely replaced with glee.

"Well," Adrian said, taking in a deep breath as he leaned against the car door. "It's your family. How do you think that went?"

Natalia looked over her shoulder to make sure her entire family wasn't standing at the door to gawk. To her surprise, no one was visible, so she pulled Adrian in for a kiss.

"Wow," he said, blinking wildly. "I'll take that as it went very well. Your family seems great, too, though I hope they won't just grab me for a kiss so aggressively."

He laughed, and she heard all the tension fade that had surely built up during the intense questioning he had just endured.

"Yeah, they're crazy, but they're mine."

"Seems like everyone gets along. Don't take that for granted."

Adrian had mentioned before the struggles of dealing with divorced parents. Even though they hadn't split until his junior year of high school, it still fractured the regularity of his life.

"I won't," Natalia said. "Seriously, though, what do you think of everyone?"

"Honestly, they remind me of my family before everything turned south. Your mom was very welcoming, and your dad is hilarious. And your siblings seem like typical younger siblings."

Natalia laughed, drunk with elation. She didn't use the word often, but the night had turned out simply perfect.

To top it off, a full moon glowed over her neighborhood, casting romance into the air.

"I'm looking forward to seeing you again," Adrian said. "You're incredible. And beautiful."

Natalia felt the muscles in her face form into a smile. They were becoming sore from doing just that several times over the past couple of hours.

The future suddenly looked clearer for Natalia. She wanted Adrian in it. They had an awkward past, but she could no longer deny the warmth she felt by his simple hello. She actually *wanted* to go to work every morning, just because he would be there.

She *needed* him. Nothing else mattered.

CHAPTER
Twenty-Eight

THEY DIALED up their relationship over the next week. The thought of spending even five minutes apart seemed grueling.

They went to lunch each day they worked together, scarfing down their food so they could head to the parking lot to make out in one of their cars for the rest of the hour. Their passion morphed into an electric storm, hotter than a summer afternoon in Phoenix.

The stares they exchanged while in the call center were concealed in secrecy and intensity. Like they were the only two people in an intertwined universe. Nothing else mattered. No one else mattered. They had just struck gold, the purest form of luck to actually find the one person in existence to spend the rest of their forever with.

Why am I even thinking such wild thoughts? It's too soon to use that heartbreaking F-word. Forever.

No matter how much she tried to remove these thoughts from mind, they returned with a determined vengeance. If she heard that F-word, she only thought of one thing.

Him.

I know it's too soon for such long-term thoughts, but when you know, *does logic take a raincheck? With love, we set up rules for ourselves to follow, then break them to find that forever person. It's never the one we think we want by setting our parameters. It's the one who slips through the cracks of judgement and pre-determined biases, and shocks us, and flares up our souls.*

"Good morning," Adrian said as he entered the call center, a general greeting to everyone. He smiled at Natalia while he crossed the room and dropped his belongings at his desk. He had made it a daily routine to first stop by the water cooler to fill up his bottle.

"Hey," Natalia whispered, the call center dead silent while their colleagues struggled to wake up.

"Why, hello there," he said with a tight-lipped grin. "How was your night?"

"Pretty good. You?"

"Was alright. Someone's car alarm went off around three o'clock, and I swear it was right outside my window. I'm a little more tired than usual."

Adrian had never made secret how much he dreaded mornings. Having his sleep interrupted did nothing to help.

His work phone rang, and he rolled his eyes to the back of his head before returning to his desk to answer it. Melissa appeared at the water cooler to fill her cup, saying nothing, but shooting a wink in Natalia's direction.

She shook her head once Melissa disappeared back to her desk. Keeping their relationship secret seemed more trivial with each passing day. She no longer cared what their coworkers would think. She wanted the world to know she had found love. What was there to be ashamed of?

Adrian finished his call, gulped half of his water bottle, and returned to the water cooler. Others started receiving calls, providing background noise so they could converse somewhat normally.

"You're gonna make yourself pee all day if you keep coming to fill up your water," Natalia said.

"Worth it. I guess you're good for my health."

Natalia's heart fluttered. Adrian always knew the right thing to say, even in the office where they had to exhibit self-control and keep their hands to themselves.

"I want to see you," Adrian said. "We haven't gone out in what? A week?"

Natalia laughed. "It's only been two days since we went to the movies."

"That's right, so like a week."

"You better go sit down before you get us both in trouble."

"Let them try."

Adrian lowered his head just below the level of the partitions, grabbed Natalia's hand, and kissed it before spinning around and returning to his desk. They spent the rest of the morning swapping text messages, making plans for their next date night, which Adrian was pushing for tomorrow.

The morning flew by, and they found the lunch hour had arrived. Adrian and Natalia made their way down to the break room to grab their lunches out of the fridge. Denver strolled in and saw them sitting together at the round table in the corner of the room.

"Hey," he said. "Just the two people I was looking for."

"Hey, Denver," Adrian said, pulling out the open chair next to him. "Come have a seat."

"Thanks." He shuffled over gingerly, thanks to a bad knee, and sat down with a plastic grocery bag filled with his food.

"Hey, Denver," Natalia said, taking her Hot Pocket out of its sleeve. "How's it going?"

"Pretty good." He paused and looked around before leaning in closer and speaking in a hushed tone. "Are the two of you dating?"

Adrian laughed. "Who wants to know?"

"Well, me, dummy, that's why I'm asking." Denver chuckled.

Adrian looked at Natalia, who only shrugged back. With their eyes locked, they made their first attempt at non-verbal communication, and Natalia believed they landed on the same page during the exchange.

"As a matter of fact," Adrian said. "Yes, we are."

"Heh. I knew it."

"How?" Natalia demanded, her voice not nearly as playful as Denver's.

"Don't get mad at me." Denver pointed a finger between them. "It's you two who aren't hiding it. I've lived on this planet a long time. You think I don't know the obvious signs of two people in love?"

"I wouldn't say we're in *love*," Adrian said. "We've only been dating for a few weeks."

"Have you really, or did this start in Vegas? Because that was almost two months ago."

"That's not the point."

Denver tossed his hands up. "I'm not here to argue with you. You may not know it yet, but you two are definitely in love. I've seen the way you look at each other. You think you're being slick, but you're not. But don't worry. You're both good looking, driven, and two of the best people I know. It would be a crime for you to refuse even the chance to see what can become of it. Your secret's safe with me."

Melissa entered the break room. "And me." She giggled deviously. "We talking about you two love-birds?"

Adrian couldn't help but laugh. Perhaps love was in the air and Natalia hadn't realized just how palpable it had become.

"Melissa knows too?" Denver asked, shaking his head. "I would've thought I'd be the first to know, seeing how I only arranged the trip that started it all. What am I, chopped liver?"

"We were going to tell you," Natalia said. "But we've been trying to keep it a secret."

"Well, you've done a terrible job, like I said. Even Lopez was asking me if I knew anything. Told him I didn't, but that's when I started paying more attention. I figured it out for myself. But don't worry, I'm not gonna tell Lopez a thing. Let him solve his own puzzles."

"I agree," Melissa said. "But you need to know the word's

going to get out soon enough. If me and Denver figured it out, others will too. And once one of the blabbermouths find out, the entire organization will know."

Natalia and Adrian exchanged another glance. Was this perfectly—or so they thought—constructed mirage all about to crumble? Or had their connection blossomed into something too powerful to cover up? An elephant in the room, covered with a drape, fooled no one.

Was there a switch that gets flicked on when it's time for a relationship to grow into something more than dating? Or did it evolve, like a tree spreading its roots over time before sprouting from the earth?

"I'm not sure what else we can do," Natalia said. "We can completely shun each other—again—but I don't see what that solves."

"I guess that's for you both to figure out," Denver said. "But I can tell you that no one is going to think it's a big deal. There will be some excitement, sure, and probably some questions about how long it's been going on. And keep in mind, these will be from everyone else on the team, not management. But after a couple of days it will become old news, and people will move on to the next thing to gossip about. You guys aren't the first relationship to come out of the call center, and you won't be the last. So as long as you don't make a big deal out of it, no one else will, either."

"I'll catch up with y'all," Melissa said, giving a quick hug to Adrian and Natalia at the same time. "So happy for you two." She left the break room without another word.

"So you think we should just be ourselves?" Adrian asked Denver.

"You should always be yourselves. No point in hiding the truth. There isn't a rule that you can't date a coworker. It might be frowned upon in some circles, but they can't fire you over it. They can't even write you up. And if Natalia is leaving soon, none of it even matters. Go on with your lives. Your time here at the Rockies is only a minor blip that you'll look back on one day."

"Thanks, Denver. It means a lot hearing that."

"No problem. Anyway, I didn't come here to actually talk about all of this with you. I just wanted to see what you guys are doing on Friday night."

"What is Friday?" Natalia asked. "The eighth?"

Denver nodded. "Yep. April eighth."

She looked at Adrian, who shrugged in return. "I don't believe we have anything planned for this weekend."

He said we, Natalia thought, her heart skipping a beat. *He's talking about* our *plans.*

"Good," Denver said. "I have a couple of extra hockey tickets to the Colorado Avalanche game. Would like to take you both. Can even grab dinner at D'Corazon before we head down."

"That sounds great," Adrian said, grinning widely.

"Count me in, too," Natalia added.

"Perfect," Denver said. "It's a date. Should be a good time—I got some really good seats. We'll head down right after work."

Denver stood up and scooted his chair in.

"Thanks, Denver," Natalia said as he started to leave.

"It's my pleasure. I should head back to work before Lopez starts crying."

Denver let out one more laugh before vanishing around the corner.

"Well, this whole thing is circling around us now," Natalia said to Adrian.

"I suppose you can only keep things like this a secret for so long. We're running out of time."

"I guess we need to finally figure out what we *are,* then we'll just continue as that."

"I agree. But it's not something I really want to discuss during our lunch break. Or even inside this building."

"Same. We should discuss it while on a date, far away from here."

Natalia laughed. It seemed inevitable they would soon make their relationship exclusive in the coming days. Neither of them wanted to scale things back, so the only direction left to go was forward.

"So the Avs game," Adrian said, cocking an eyebrow. "Do you even like hockey?"

"Not really."

"Me neither. I used to follow it, but haven't in about ten years. I know how the game works, and should know most of the rules, assuming they haven't changed them."

"Good enough for me. As long as we're there together, I know we'll have a blast."

CHAPTER *Twenty-Nine*

WHEN FRIDAY ROLLED AROUND, one of those warm spring days that better resembled summer graced the city of Denver. Baseball season was underway. Not a cloud danced across the crisp blue sky, and the business crowd packed into the bars at five o'clock to enjoy their escape from the winter gloom. Even if more snow would likely fall later in the month—spring time in Denver suffered the same mood swings as a two-year-old child not getting their way—that couldn't hinder the euphoria of this particular Friday evening.

Denver had gotten off work at four o'clock and headed down to the restaurant to wait for Adrian and Natalia, who both got off at five.

The two had a brief discussion about whether they should drive down to the arena and deal with parking, or just walk, meaning they'd have to walk back after the hockey game ended after ten o'clock.

They agreed to walk. That only meant more time together before having to say goodnight.

Once the clock struck five, they had at least the next several hours together, and with a trusted friend who now knew their secret. They had nothing to hide, and could even hold hands the entire time during the hockey game if they wanted.

It was freeing to not have to conceal their adoration for each other, even if for one night.

Maybe this is the night we'll agree to bring our relationship public, Natalia wondered as she changed out of her work clothes into something more comfortable for the evening ahead.

Even if it wasn't, she didn't care. Her life was in a groove. She had actually landed a third interview with a company that expressed a genuine interest in hiring her. And they were in downtown Denver.

She finished changing and stepped out of the break room's bathroom, finding Adrian at the Coke vending machine, grabbing two cans for their hike down Blake Street.

"You ready?" he asked, a charming grin as he stuck out the can to Natalia.

"Absolutely, just let me go put my bag under my desk and we can head out."

Three minutes later, they were walking hand-in-hand down the sidewalk, fitting in like any other couple they passed by. Natalia still couldn't wrap her mind around how natural everything felt and flowed with Adrian. It was nearly impossible to remember just how much she had once hated him. The mere thought made her queasy. She never wanted to feel such a negative emotion toward him again and had little reason to expect she ever would.

"Beautiful evening," Adrian said once they were just a block away from the restaurant.

"It really is. I love the energy that comes with warmer weather. Plants aren't the only thing that comes back to life—I think we all do a little."

"Good point. Even though I'd much rather be a bear and take a six-month nap."

Natalia laughed, then leaned over to peck him on the cheek.

"What was that for?" he asked, smiling out one side of his mouth.

"Just because. Is that okay?" She nudged him in the side.

"Always."

He wrapped his hand around her waist while they entered a bustling D'Corazon. Servers scurried in every direction, large trays of Mexican food in hand, the sizzling from a couple of fajita dishes screaming over the elevated white noise of everyone speaking. Laughter filled the building as glasses clinked against one another.

They found Denver sitting alone at a table along the wall, guarding the chips and salsa like someone had threatened to take them away.

"'Sup," he said, hesitantly pushing the bowl of chips back to the center of the table. He was already halfway through a margarita.

"Denver!" Adrian said, pulling out the two seats for him and Natalia. "I guess we need to catch up to you." He nodded toward the margarita.

Denver studied his margarita, then took another long sip. "That you do. You know, the Rio across the street gets all the hype for their margaritas, but I think these are way better. No cheap booze dumped into it just to get you drunk. This is the good stuff. Top shelf. You know what, first round's on me."

He waved over their server and ordered three more margaritas.

Adrian and Natalia sat next to each other across from Denver. She felt his leg rubbing calmly against hers and didn't bother analyzing what it might mean. It didn't matter. The night would be magical—that much she knew.

"Long week, huh?" Denver said. "The week after Opening Day is always a grind. We're coming down from the craziness, but the fans keep calling in to buy more tickets. Goes like that every season."

"Indeed, it was chaos," Natalia said. She hadn't told anyone about the third interview she had lined up next week, not even Adrian. It had reached the point she didn't want to jinx anything, seeing how the past few had fizzled into the abyss.

"Wasn't too bad," Adrian said, his bouncing knee now rubbing against Natalia's thigh. She reached under the table and put a calming hand on it, and he stopped immediately, returning the favor by placing his hand on her knee.

"You two excited for the game?" Denver asked.

"Yes," Adrian said. "I haven't been to an Avs game in years. Not since I was a teenager."

"I'm not sure I've ever been to one," Natalia said. "Not that I remember."

"I like hockey," Denver said. "Not as much as baseball or football, but I'll watch it when the Avs are doing good. Sadly, they're not this year. I think that's why I was given these tickets. We're gonna be three rows off the glass, right behind the Avs bench."

Natalia's eyebrows shot up. "Wow."

"Exactly. One hell of a way to enjoy your first game."

"I'll say. How did you get these tickets, anyway?" Natalia asked as she dipped a chip into the salsa.

"I make lots of friends from the other teams in town. I know we're not supposed to, but I trade tickets. It's one of those rules that even the higher-ups break. You know they're not paying for suite tickets at the Broncos games. They all scratch each other's backs, and I do the same. Gave my two tickets away for next Saturday's Rockies game to land these for tonight."

"I've done that before," Adrian said, nodding along. "Been able to sit on the field for a lacrosse game with the Outlaws. I've been trying to get a basketball connection over at the Nuggets, but haven't been able to yet."

"It takes time. You just gotta network."

"Well, we definitely appreciate you thinking of us," Natalia said.

"Of course. My new favorite couple."

The words made Natalia's heart race. Adrian's leg started

bouncing again, like a bunny on drugs. He even looked around, like he had just remembered they were supposed to keep it a secret.

"Tell me something," Denver continued. "Now that the truth is out and we're not in the office. How much of a role did the Vegas trip play in this happening?"

He leaned back and waited for an answer.

Adrian and Natalia exchanged a glance before she laughed and responded. "It played a huge part. I'll be the first to admit I had no interest in going once I found out Adrian was going to be there. I even looked for ways out, but couldn't do that to Caroline. Once we were there, though, everything changed. We were forced to spend time together, and it was so laid back we could put aside our differences and just get to know each other. I'd say the Vegas trip was where we became friends."

Adrian nodded in agreement.

"Well, a strong friendship is the best foundation for any long-term relationship," Denver said. "I guess I'll take the credit for putting you together. Just change my name to Cupid."

They all laughed.

"We thought you might think that," Adrian said. "And I suppose, to some extent, you're right. I thought we were just going to Vegas to welcome me to the real world of being of age. It ended up being so much more."

"One day you two will go back there together, and you'll remember it as the place where it all started. Vegas isn't the most romantic place, but it will be for you."

Natalia loved hearing someone talk about their relationship in such a positive light. He was even talking about the *future*, as if it was guaranteed they'd be together for a long time.

"I hope you're right," Adrian said, and the words couldn't sound any more genuine.

"I know these things," Denver said. "Not to put pressure on you, but you have what it takes to make this last. That might sound crazy this early in your dating, but it's true."

Their server stopped by with the drinks and took their dinner order.

"Cheers," Denver said, raising his glass. "To friendship."

They knocked their glasses together and dove into the margaritas.

"I gotta ask," Adrian said. "Did you plan for this all to happen in Vegas?"

Denver snickered. "Of course not. I only invited Caroline because I know she loves Vegas and gets free flights. When she invited Natalia, I thought it was a good idea. Give me some rest while you went out on the town."

"Did you know something was going on once we were all there?" Natalia asked.

Denver nodded. "Of course. Caroline noticed, too. It's no secret you two didn't get along at work. After two days in Vegas, you were actually speaking like normal people do. I didn't think you'd necessarily fall for each other, but it was obvious you were becoming friends. And you didn't realize it."

"Oh, we realized it," Adrian said. "We had a long talk about what was going on between us. Cleared the air of the past."

"Well, good. You should always do that. With everyone. You see where it led you just this one time. Imagine capturing that with everyone in your life."

"I don't think I could handle that with so many people," Adrian said with a subtle shake of the head.

"I'm not saying you need to create a long-lasting friendship with everyone you meet. Far from it. Just approach each person the way you two approached your opportunity in Vegas. See, one thing I've learned is that people will come and go. Friends, lovers, even family. It's like a carousel. We only have so much bandwidth to maintain high levels of connection with those in our life. But don't let that take away from creating something special in the moment. I look at all you college kids in the call center and you get along so well. You have a real, genuine friendship with each other. But that doesn't mean it will last forever. In fact, I'd say ninety percent of your friendships in the call center will fizzle out."

"It's hard to believe that," Adrian said.

Denver nodded. "It should be that way. That means you're making the most out of your time together. You're not worried about what comes next, or where the finish line is. You enjoy each other's company. But life changes. You'll all go your separate ways once you find new jobs. Some of you will get married and start families, others won't. Those differences will cause the friendships to fade, but that has no bearing on the present. Right now, you're all in the same stage of life. You haven't reached that split yet."

"I guess that makes a little sense," Natalia said.

"Work friends are a funny thing. They really can become your best friends, even like family. But don't lose sight that those friendships are only flourishing because you spend so much time together. Eight hours every day. That's literally more time than you spend with your actual family. But once you remove the job, that's when the reality of the friendship gets tested. See, they thrive in the first place because of convenience. You're forced to sit in a room with these people and go through the grind together. It creates a natural bond. When people leave the job, that bond is broken. Some will remain friends, but that's because the connection goes so much beyond work. Like you two. Natalia will get a new job soon, but you'll make it a priority to keep seeing each other. You don't need to be together in the office to keep things afloat. You weren't even at work when you two started to know each other."

As true as it was, Natalia still dreaded the thought of *not* seeing Adrian for those eight hours every day.

"Your generation has it much different, though," Denver continued. "When I left a job, that was the last time I'd see or hear from my coworkers, minus the one or two who would actually stick around. Today, you're all on social media. Even if you don't speak to each other, you're still connected and know what's going on in each other's lives. And I think that's kind of cool. I'd have loved something like that when I was younger."

The server interrupted Denver by bringing their dishes to the table. Before they started eating, Adrian said, "Well, Denver, I really appreciate your insight into everything. It means a lot. I can only hope to be so wise when I'm your age."

Denver laughed. "Wise, huh? I'll take it. I've just seen how things repeat themselves throughout my life, and figure there's a pattern to it. Better to be equipped by knowing what's coming next. I've sat in the call center for the past ten years. Every two seasons usually bring a whole new batch of college students in need of part-time work. And every group comes together for that little time together, and then they go their separate ways. I like to think of the call center as an on-ramp to the rest of your life. And there's nothing wrong with that. It's a crappy job, but if you get to do it with your best friends every day, it's not really so bad, is it?"

Natalia reached back under the table and grabbed Adrian's hand, squeezing it, *grateful* for it. "It really isn't."

CHAPTER *Thirty*

THE HOCKEY GAME passed in a blur. They shared laughs all night. The arena was rather empty. It was the second-to-last home game of what had been a miserable season for the Avalanche. During timeouts and intermissions, Adrian's leg bounced wildly out of control, as if he was longing to sprint a mile. Natalia considered analyzing the meaning of such a jittery movement, but didn't need to go down any rabbit holes. Not tonight. Everything was going so perfect.

Denver's speech at dinner had left an impression on them. It was uplifting, motivational, and a bit frightening. Natalia had never put so much thought into her future and how her existing relationships would all play out. Hearing Denver make bold predictions—ones she couldn't really argue against the logic—made her cherish her remaining time at the call center. And more importantly, her time with Adrian every day.

It was something they had both been taking for granted, and wouldn't any more.

Denver had offered to drive them back to the Coors Field parking lot once the game ended, but they declined, opting to have those extra few minutes together.

And so they strolled down the sidewalks of a now bustling

downtown Denver. The business crowds had given way to the twenty-somethings out to party the Friday night away.

They held hands, people-watching, not a ton of conversation taking place.

"You seem quiet," Natalia said, noting her own silence. Adrian's hand had the slightest of trembles. "Is something wrong?"

Adrian shook his head. "Nothing at all."

He didn't elaborate and fell silent as they walked the next block. Natalia sensed the energy from Adrian had changed, yet she couldn't pinpoint to what exactly. Should she continue to prod, or just let him be? Something was definitely bothering him. Why couldn't he share?

They had two blocks remaining until they would arrive at the parking lot to go their separate ways, and she didn't want the night to end in such a strange mood. She observed him as they walked, and he kept his gaze ahead, staring into the distance. He had the look of someone with hundreds of thoughts running through his mind, so she decided on a different approach.

"What are you thinking about?" she asked, swinging their arms together.

The question brought him out of his daydream, but not enough. His arm started to waver. *Something* was bothering him.

"Just some things." His voice was uninterested. Distant.

"Okay? Is there a reason you're not wanting to talk to me? It seems weird after we had such a fun night together."

"It's not that I don't want to talk to you. I'm just processing some things."

A quick flame of anger flickered within Natalia. Another vague answer. Why?

"I thought we'd reached a point where we feel comfortable telling each other anything," she said. "Or am I mistaken?"

Adrian shook his head, eyes staring ahead, but not looking at anything in particular. "That's not it."

He said nothing else, and her concern was quickly turning into agitation.

Did something Denver said spark second thoughts for Adrian? He was still only two months removed from his last relationship. Was he having doubt about ending that and rushing into the next one so quickly?

Now Natalia's mind became a tangled mess, furthering her frustration. She even teetered on the brink of nervousness. Part of her wanted to stall and not go back to their cars for fear of what he might say.

What are you contemplating inside that mind of yours?

Since they had started dating, Adrian had been a fairly open book, happy to share everything about his past and his dreams for the future. Why shut down all the sudden, unless something was wrong?

They reached the stairs that descended from the sidewalk to the parking lot, and she let go of Adrian's hand with a forceful gesture of whipping it away like she had just touched a hot stove.

"What's wrong?" Adrian asked, staring at his hand like it had done something to her.

"You're not talking to me. That's what's wrong. See how I did that? Something is bothering me, and I used my words to explain it to you."

Natalia gritted her teeth.

Adrian smiled, but his legs were visibly quivering.

"Oh, so you think this is funny?" Natalia snarled.

"Yes, actually, I do," he replied with a nervous chuckle. "C'mon."

Adrian reached out for Natalia's hand, and after a few seconds of her staring at it, she reluctantly grabbed it. They continued down the stairs.

"Nothing is wrong at all," Adrian said, more poised and calm. "But we do need to talk."

Natalia's jaw fell. "I know you didn't just drop those words on me."

Adrian's grin widened. "I did."

They reached the bottom landing and Adrian pulled her

toward their two cars parked next to each other, stopping in front of Natalia's. He released her hand, prompting her to cross her arms as she leaned against the front bumper.

"Well?" she said, jutting her head out. "What are we talking about?"

An odd mixture of nerves and excitement swirled within her stomach. She didn't *think* he was going to call things off right now, but she needed to protect herself and not eliminate the possibility. She had no idea what was about to come out of his mouth.

"These past two months have truly meant so much to me," Adrian said.

Natalia's pounding heart sunk a level lower. Adrian's tone had the delicacy of someone about to deliver bad news.

"Looking in from the outside," he continued, staring at the ground. "The whole thing seems a little ridiculous, right? We used to despise each other. We were both in serious relationships just two months ago. Did we rush into this too soon? I suppose we'll never know what the 'correct' way to transition from one relationship to the next is. Maybe it all depends on who's involved."

"What are you getting at?!" Natalia was losing control over her emotions. They were spiking up and down like she was on a wild roller coaster.

"I love you," Adrian said, his smile softening around the corners. The words whipped Natalia across the face. She hadn't known what to expect, but it definitely wasn't *that*.

She leaped up from her car and threw her arms open. "You *love* me?"

Adrian nodded. "I know it seems crazy to say this already. But I can't help how I feel. I wouldn't have said it if I didn't think you already felt the same way. I love you, and I want to be with you. Only you."

Natalia's throat grew dry. Not only did Adrian make the ultimate confession, he believed she felt the same. Did she?

Attracted to him? Yes. Enjoy spending time with him? More

than anything. Did she have an interest in dating anyone else? None at all.

But did that all equal love?

Wasn't love nothing more than a blind leap of faith?

She never believed love was an emotion like joy or sadness, but a choice. You chose who you loved. Chose to spread love in the world. It was never forced.

Natalia swallowed the lump that had ballooned in her throat, a smile taking over her face beyond her control. "I love you, too."

She watched the relief swim across Adrian's eyes as he lunged forward and pulled her into his embrace, running a hand up and down her back as their heads rested against each other.

He pulled back just enough to kiss her, and this time, it felt different. A magical glee exploded when their lips connected. Her heart drummed madly, and she felt Adrian's doing the same as she rested a hand on his chest.

They pulled apart and stared into each other's souls, electricity burning in those few inches between their faces.

Natalia licked her lips, still tasting Adrian on them. "What do we do now?"

The smile hadn't left Adrian's face. "We take Denver's advice. Let's be ourselves. No more secrets. Nothing to hide. I love you and you love me, and we shouldn't have any reason to hide that."

Natalia nodded, happy tears welling in her eyes. "Okay. Monday will be interesting."

"Who cares? Let's enjoy tonight—we have a cause for celebration. Ice cream?"

"Okay."

"I know a spot. Follow me."

He kissed her again before hurrying around to get in his car.

She hopped in hers and they raced across town to Little Man Ice Cream.

During the drive over, Natalia couldn't control her thoughts. She had been taken on such a ride over the past hour; her mind was still struggling to completely process everything.

"I love Adrian," she said, needing to hear the words leave her lips. He was right. None of it made sense for why they should have ended up together. Last summer, she would have been offended at the idea of even going on a date with him. Now she couldn't imagine ever dating anyone else.

They parked and crossed the street to the ice cream stand, ordering their cones and finding an open table under the warm night sky.

Adrian raised his cone in the air. "To love."

Natalia followed suit, grinning as she stared across the table, tapping her ice cream cone against his. "To love."

Epilogue

10 YEARS LATER…

"Finish up your sandwich, then we can get dessert," Natalia said to their oldest child, Andrea.

The family of five basked in the shade under a park tree, three blankets sprawled out, the picnic basket now empty of the chips, sandwiches, and juice boxes that sat in front of them all.

"But Mommy, I don't like the lettuce on my sandwich," Andrea whined. She was six years old and carving out her own personality and preferences.

"Tough. No dessert until you eat all of it. How's my little mister doing?"

"You'd think we never feed him," Adrian said, sitting next to their four-year-old son, Francisco. "Right, dude?"

Francisco laughed, stuffing the last of his veggie chips into his mouth.

"And how's the little one doing?" Adrian asked, nodding to their youngest, a two-year-old girl named Sabrina.

"Only eating the chips," Natalia said, playfully rolling her eyes. "I think she's taken two bites of the sandwich."

"Sounds about right."

Sabrina cackled in delight, and Natalia wondered if toddlers were the true geniuses of the world. They seemed to get away with whatever they wanted, and could simply laugh it off with a surprising cuteness.

"Mommy," Francisco said. "I don't like the salad."

"It's called lettuce, and it's good for you. Stop copying your sister and eat."

She stared at Adrian and bulged her eyes in that look only parents exchanged when their kids ran them through the daily test of emotional control.

He smiled back in response, always there to calm the mood when things got too hectic. Sure, it might take them an hour to eat half of a turkey sandwich, but what's the hurry?

Adrian had finished his lunch and shifted his focus to helping Francisco. They watched a nearby group of friends playing corn hole. A three-on-three pickup basketball game had just begun on the courts behind them. Frisbees soared in the air as dogs chased after. A woman had pulled out her violin and played for the next thirty minutes from her post on the park bench.

The perfect summer day, Natalia thought, watching her husband feed their son.

Across the street, a line of people wrapped around the block for Little Man Ice Cream. The building was a thirty-foot tall tin milk can, with three windows to walk up and place your order. It had grown in popularity since the first time Natalia had gone with Adrian ten years prior. During the summer months, the line always wrapped around the block, even sometimes in the winter.

"Why did we have to come all the way to this park?" Andrea asked with her six-year-old sass. "We have a park by our house."

Adrian laughed.

"This is a special place for me and Mommy," he explained. "See, our love story kind of started here. Well, Vegas, I suppose, but we came here after we first said we love each other."

"Yuck." Andrea's face squirmed into an expression like she had eaten something nasty.

"Yuck," Francisco copied, prompting a round of laughter.

"What's a Vegas?" Andrea asked.

"It's a city in a different state. We'll take you there when you're *much* older. Now, finish your food so we can go get some ice cream."

Andrea fell silent and begrudgingly took her next nibble.

"Any update on that news you're expecting?" Natalia asked Adrian.

"Not yet."

After several years of slogging through corporate jobs, Adrian had decided to finally pursue his dream of becoming an author. With ten books published, he was on the verge of getting to leave his job behind and start a full-time career writing books. They were waiting for word back from an audiobook production company about picking up one of his series. The advance money that had been discussed would be more than enough for Adrian to take that leap.

"I'm sure soon enough," Natalia said. "Don't worry about it."

He nodded and offered a forced smile. She knew the prospect was causing him so much angst, yet there was nothing she could do beyond giving words of support.

Deep down, she knew the publishers would sign the book deal. They had to. Everything had played out so smoothly in their life together. That deal would be their ticket to a new chapter.

"I'm not worried," he replied, shooting a wink across the picnic blanket.

Natalia often thought back to how all of this had fallen into place and still struggled to believe it sometimes. When she looked across at the man she had fallen so madly in love with, the hatred she had once felt toward him seemed as foreign as a language she had never heard.

One trip to Vegas that was meant to be nothing more than a celebration had changed the entire trajectory of their lives. She still trembled at the thought of what her life would look like today had she not agreed to go on that trip. Would she still be married with three incredible children? It was possible, but she doubted if her heart would feel the same.

Stop thinking like that. It all worked out.

She thought back to Denver's insights that night of the Avalanche game. Now, ten years deeper into life and with three little people looking to her for guidance all the time, his words never rang truer. Whether friends or family, only a select few stayed in your life forever.

Beyond that, she realized, the same applied for places and situations. Life was nothing but multiple threads being constantly woven, all to set up something further down the road. What would the final product look like after all those threads connected? No one could ever know.

Adrian had a lifelong love for baseball and once dreamed to work in the industry. Natalia cared much less about baseball and just wanted an employment that would work around her school schedule. Her aunt, who she couldn't even recall the last time she had spoken with, just happened to work for the Rockies, too.

With that, two unrelated threads started to intertwine. But so much more chance had to fall into place. Neither Adrian nor Natalia controlled the seating arrangement in the call center. Adrian ended up next to Denver, Natalia next to Caroline. Friendships flourished from there, twisting the threads closer together without either of them knowing.

Had either of them sat on the opposite side of the office, would they still be sharing a beautiful picnic in the park right now? Two people meeting each other and falling in love required hundreds of *billions* of moving parts to all fall perfectly into place. Looking back on it, so little was actually controlled by the two involved lovers.

Fate. Destiny. Whatever you want to call it, there was no denying the mystery shrouding true love.

"Anyone home?" Adrian asked, his voice snapping her out of her daydream.

Natalia shook her head, startled. "I'm sorry. What?"

Adrian laughed. "You okay? You looked totally zoned out."

"I'm great."

"I was asking if you want us to pack up and all head across the street. Or I can go with Andrea and we can bring back the ice cream here."

"Let's stay here, don't you think? We have the perfect spot."

"Great. Andrea just finished while you were staring into outer space. Let's go."

Adrian reached out his hand toward their oldest daughter, and she grasped it with such excitement to be crossing the street to the giant milk can.

"Hey," Natalia said, grabbing Adrian by the arm before he started away, pulling him in toward her face. "I love you."

They kissed, and even after ten years, the fires of passion still burned deep within her soul.

"Ewwww!" Andrea said, squeezing her eyes shut, jerking her head side to side in sheer disgust.

Adrian and Natalia laughed before he stood back up. "Enough of that. I just love your mother. If that's okay with you."

"I guess," Andrea said, planting her hands on her hips. "Just stop kissing all the time."

"I'll see what I can do. Now, let's go get some ice cream for everyone."

Francisco started a chant, "Ice cream! Ice cream! Ice cream!"

Sabrina copied him in her young, slurred speech.

And Natalia lay down on the blanket, planting her elbow on the ground to rest her head in her hand. She watched as Adrian walked away with Andrea, knowing her life couldn't be any more perfect.

Please Review

We hope you enjoyed *A Twist of Hate*
by TE Lorenzo.
If you did, we would ask that you please
rate and review this title.
Every review helps our authors.

Rate and Review: A Twist of Hate

Meet The Author

TE Lorenzo is the debut author of A Twist of Hate. Having lived through his own enemies-to-lovers story, he believes love can come from the most unexpected of places. When he's not writing, TE is likely chasing his kids around, playing baseball, or relaxing with a good book. He is currently living out his happily-ever-after with his wife and three kids in their hometown of Denver, CO.

Other Titles from 5 Prince Publishing

Christmas Cove *Sarah Dressler*
Firewall *Jessica Mehring*
Vampires of Atlantis *Courtney Davis*
Composing Laney *S.E. Reichert*
Liz's Road Trip *Bernadette Marie*
Back to the 80s *S.E. Reichert & Kerrie Flanagan*
Granting Katelyn *S.E. Reichert*
Ghosts of Alda *Russell Archey*
The Serpent and the Firefly *Courtney Davis*
Raising Elle *S.E. Reichert*
Rom Com Movie Club No.3 *Bernadette Marie*
Rom Com Movie Club No.2 *Bernadette Marie*
Rom Com Movie Club No.1 *Bernadette Marie*
A Crossbow Christmas *Ann Swann*
Hot For Teacher *Felicia Carparelli*
The Happily Ever After Bookstore *Bernadette Marie*
Perfect Mrs Claus *Barbara Matteson*
Princess of Prias *Courtney Davis*
Paige and the Reluctant Artist *Darci Garcia*
A Spider in the Garden *Courtney Davis*
Megan's Choice *Darci Garcia*

www.ingramcontent.com/pod-product-compliance
Lightning Source LLC
LaVergne TN
LVHW091135080826
845145LV00008B/2166